Tom: To Secure His Legacy

Tom: To Secure His Legacy

Mansfield Park Continuation, Episode 4

LEENIE BROWN

LEENIE B BOOKS
HALIFAX

Cover design by Leenie B Books. Images sourced from Deposit Photos and Period Images.

Tom: To Secure His Legacy © 2019 Leenie Brown. All Rights Reserved, except where otherwise noted.

ISBN (print) 978-1-989410-09-7; (ebook) 978-1-989410-08-0

Contents

Dear Reader,

At the end of *Mansfield Park*, Jane Austen wrote:

> *Let other pens dwell on guilt and misery. I quit such odious subjects as soon as I can, impatient to restore everybody not greatly in fault themselves to tolerable comfort and to have done with all the rest.*

It is my goal in writing the books found in the *Other Pens Collection* to take up my pen and continue the stories of various Austen characters who were at fault in some way in Miss Austen's novels. In these stories of redemption and reformation, I do not look to dwell on the characters' guilt and misery so much as help them find a way to overcome their failures and find their own happiness.

These stories are not retellings or even variations. They are continuations, which begin with at least one Austen character and spread outward as the change from in that one individual's life influences the lives of others in his or her circle of friends and family.

The book you hold in your hand is one of my *Mansfield*

Park Continuation Episodes, which began after the close of *Manfield Park* with Henry Crawford deciding to prove himself worthy of a good woman. While each episode contains a complete happily ever after for its hero and heroine, it is assumed that the reader knows about the events in the preceding books. Therefore, while reading in any order may be done, for maximum enjoyment, reading all of the books in order is recommended.

An End and a Beginning

There was comfort also in Tom, who gradually regained his health, without regaining the thoughtlessness and selfishness of his previous habits. He was the better for ever for his illness. He had suffered, and he had learned to think: two advantages that he had never known before; and the self-reproach arising from the deplorable event in Wimpole Street, to which he felt himself accessory by all the dangerous intimacy of his unjustifiable theatre, made an impression on his mind which, at the age of six-and-twenty, with no want of sense or good companions, was durable in its happy effects. He became what he ought to be: useful to his father, steady and quiet, and not living merely for himself.

Austen, Jane. *Mansfield Park*

This is where Miss Austen left Tom and where our story begins — as he is attempting to become "what he ought to be."

Chapter 1

Morning crept its way across the room, first spilling over the windowsill and then creeping across the floor before slipping through the gap in the bed curtains.

Tom Bertram tossed an arm across his eyes to block its advance. He did not wish to wake just yet. There was a beautiful angel singing to him as she blotted his face with a cool cloth, and if he waited just a moment longer, he might be able to open his eyes in his dream and finally see her face.

He groaned. It was no use.

His angel had flown away once again, and he was left with only a memory of her voice.

He stretched and slowly rose to a sitting position. He needed to get dressed and start his day. He knew he needed to, but he had little desire to do so. Being responsible was far less enjoyable than being reckless.

He groaned again as he straightened his leg. Being reckless did come with its own set of complaints. His leg hurt less than it used to, but it was still a trial. Thankfully, according to the physician, the break had knit together as it should. However, the leg was still not as strong as Tom would like it to be, and it did ache rather a lot in the mornings after being motionless for so long as he slept.

He pushed his way out of his covers and, taking up the cane that stood next to his bed, he rose. Within half an hour's time, he would be able to rise without the use of the blasted thing, but first thing in the morning, he could not. It was as if his muscles protested rising more than his brain did.

After pulling the bell for his man, Tom began what he could of his ablutions while waiting.

"Your paper is waiting for you below," his valet said as he entered the room.

Reading the paper first thing in the morning, just like rising while it was still morning, was new for Tom. Being a respectable and responsible gentleman seemed to have many unsavoury costs. However, if he wished to recover even part of what he had lost of his and his brother's inheritance in his dissolute days, he must learn the part of a duty-bound gentleman. It was not his natural bent. It should be, but it was not.

He lifted his chin so that his man could complete his shaving.

It would likely be easier to face both the morning and his future prospects with greater equanimity if he had gone to bed at an earlier hour.

He chuckled to himself. Was that not what his father always scolded? *Tom, a baronet does not while away his hours in pleasure to the harm of his estate.* That was a lesson hard learned.

Tom dried his face and began the work of making himself presentably attired.

Before he began any study of his new gambling haunts today, he had a friend upon whom to call – a friend who was both fortunate to have survived the night and the reason for Tom's lack of rest.

It had been a late night, waiting to see if Gabe had recovered his boat. And then, there had been the time at Gabe's house while Tom had waited to hear the surgeon's evaluation of his friend's injuries.

Today promised to be one of great interest, for Gabe had promised to share the harrowing tale of his ordeal, and then...

Tom chuckled to himself as his man tied his cravat.

"Mr. Durward is planning to give up his bachelor state," Tom said to his man.

"My congratulations," his man replied.

"He is hoping to tie himself to Miss Crawford."

"Miss Crawford?" The man before him blinked. "The lady that was at Mansfield?"

Tom nodded. "The very one. Will not Edmund be shocked when I invite Mr. and Mrs. Durward for a visit someday?"

"Indeed!"

"She has changed," Tom added. "Fanny will be pleased to see the transformation. I am not certain how my brother will receive it. He is more reticent in things than his wife."

He gave himself a looking over in the mirror. He did cut a dashing figure even when he was being respectable.

"Have there been any letters from Mansfield?"

"No, sir, none yesterday and so far, none today. There were some invitations, which have been placed in your study."

Tom's least favourite room in his entire life had been the study. He still had to remind himself not to shudder at the word.

The study here in town was his, and his alone. His father had given him sole control of this town house after Tom had recovered from his illness ready to take on a new life – one that was not given over to pleasure. Therefore, this study, since it was his and his alone, did not have to be one of criticism and scolding. This study could be an agreeable and even friendly place.

He loved his father, but theirs was not a close relationship. He would not be as his father was. He would attempt to encourage his children to do well, of course, but not in the same way his father had. He would smile and praise his children from the beginning rather than waiting until one of them had been lost to her willful ways and another had nearly killed himself trying to be as unlike his father as was humanly possible.

"Would you see that some breakfast is sent to me in my study?"

"Of course, sir."

"And the paper," he called after his man.

He blew out a breath. It was time to begin in earnest his work of recouping his losses, although he had to admit that he was not entirely certain he understood all the workings of investing. Gabe would likely be able to help him find places to put his money that would earn him a healthy – but secure – return.

Gambling was not new to Tom. He had lost plenty of money at card tables, races, and the like. However, speculating on shares and such was different. There was still the possibility of gain or loss, but the money he was using seemed to be somehow more valuable.

It was not, of course.

The money had not changed one wit. It was Tom who had changed. He saw things in such a different way now since his angel had saved his life those many long months ago. Perhaps if he were very fortunate, one day, he would get to see her face and thank her for her service. But for now, he would have to satisfy himself with his memories of her care and her songs.

~*~*~

After a thorough reading of the paper with a particularly close review of the financial numbers listed in it while eating his breakfast, Tom got his hat and coat and made his way from his house to Gabe's.

"Mr. Bertram," Mrs. Durward greeted him with a smile. "You must sit here." She led him to a settee near the window. She leaned toward him when he had taken his seat. "There is a footstool just to the right if your leg should need it."

He thanked her.

"You are not too cold here, are you?"

"No, no. I am perfectly comfortable."

"I have a blanket."

"If I become chilled, I will tell you."

She smiled at him and patted his knee just as she seemed to like to do to Gabe. It was as if, after having only met Tom a few days ago, she had laid claim to him as a second son.

He had to chuckle when Mr. Benjamin Waller was given nearly the same treatment. However, Mr. Waller was not offered a footstool, but brandy was available if any of his bruises were to give him too much pain.

Mr. Waller leaned toward Tom when Mrs. Durward had turned her attention to her son who was being helped into the room by a footman.

"Do not tell her about my stitches," he whispered, gingerly patting his side.

Tom's eyes grew wide.

"It was a small cut, and the surgeon thought it would heal better if sewn together. It is nothing compared to Durward's injuries." He sighed. "I did not think he would make it from the ship to the shore. He is a fortunate fellow."

Tom nodded and muttered something about Gabe's tenacity while watching that friend allow his mother, a slight woman, who could not be a hair taller than five feet, to tell him how to sit and what he needed to be well. He could see on Gabe's face that it was a trial to accept the coddling, but Gabe was not the sort to injure anyone who did not deserve injury.

"Radcliff is dead?" Tom asked Waller quietly.

Last night, Gabe had thought the man who had stolen his boat had died but was not entirely certain he remembered correctly.

Waller nodded. "One shot to his heart. It was impressive to see Mr. Durward lift that gun while he lay on the deck with Miss Crawford draped across his chest. His hand was so steady. His face..." Waller shook his head. "Anyone who saw it would think twice about ever endangering someone for whom Durward cared. There was death in his eyes. I have seen that look a few times when engaged in a battle over a ship. He was protecting her," he nodded to Miss Crawford, who had just arrived with her sister, Margaret, and her brother, Henry, "and would die doing so."

The right corner of Tom's mouth tipped up. That sounded just like Gabriel Durward. The man was fiercely loyal and just as passionate about seeing things done justly. Tom thanked providence for smiling down on him and allowing him to meet Gabe.

"I am well," Tom said in answer to Margaret Grant's inquiry before continuing his conversation with Waller.

"What of the other men?" Tom asked while continuing to watch the proceedings in the room.

Miss Crawford was being made to sit next to Gabe but nearer the fire. Apparently, Mrs. Durward thought that any lady would find it exceptionally cold today. He chuckled.

"She is very mothering." Waller nodded to Mrs. Durward.

"That she is," Tom agreed.

"The others are being held for trial," Waller said, returning to Tom's question. "All, but one, will likely see the gallows."

"All, but one?"

Waller nodded. "Miss Crawford spoke on behalf of one of the men. He helped her and her sister escape the room where they were being held, and so I suspect he will live – not in England – but his assistance will likely save his neck."

"Miss Crawford spoke for him?" She continued to surprise him with how much she seemed to have changed since her time at Mansfield.

"She was on her way down the ladder to the rowboat but then popped her head back up over the rail and told me about his assistance. She is a strong lady to have held up to her ordeal as well as she appears to have. Durward is fortunate to have found a lady of such good character."

Tom chuckled. A lady of good character was not how anyone at Mansfield would describe Miss Crawford. "She has not always been such a lady. I think it is Durward's influence, actually."

"Indeed?" Waller said in surprise.

Tom shrugged. "She needed to find herself. I would not wish to besmirch the lady, but her previous friends did nothing to encourage a noble character." He could not fault her for that. Had he not also been attempting to find himself in frivolous and reckless behavior?

He took his eyes off how Miss Crawford was ducking her head at something Gabe had said. She really was so different from who she had been at Mansfield. Even Edmund would have to be pleased to see it.

"I assume you read the report in the paper about Lady St. James's brooch?"

Waller nodded.

"It was placed in Gabe's possession by a lady who once was a friend of both Lady St. James and Miss Crawford."

"No!"

"I assure you it is true. Lady St. James is not pleased to lose her influence over Miss Crawford to the likes of Gabe." Tom leaned toward Waller. "He's in trade you know."

"I did know that." Waller chuckled. "Lady St. James, you say?"

Tom nodded just as Gabe began to tell his tale of narrowly escaping death at the hands of a Frenchman from whom he had taken a ship three years ago while under a letter of marque — a ship that he had then purchased from the prize court. Gabriel Durward knew risk and reward as well as he knew risk and loss. However, unlike Tom, who had never learned from his losses, Gabe had. He was as shrewd as he was daring. If anyone could help Tom become a financial success and rid himself of the debt he had created for Mansfield, it would be an industrious fellow like Gabe.

Be that as it may, there was something Tom must do first. He must assist Gabe as he had promised.

"I would not disagree with such a claim," Waller was saying in response to Gabe's comment about how Radcliff had been killed.

Tom stood. It was time to do his part in allowing his friend to find his happiness.

"I should likely contrive some reason to persuade you all to leave the room and allow Gabe and Miss Crawford some privacy, but I have not been able to come up with one. Therefore, I suggest we all take our leave and perhaps enjoy another cup of tea in the morning room."

With any luck, Tom thought as he closed the door to the sitting room after everyone had exited, he would one day find himself as besotted as his friend.

Chapter 2

"I do not know why you do not just spend your days in a tea room," Robert Eldridge said as he climbed into the hired hack after his sister, Faith — not that the person entering the carriage looked like a sister.

"And in gentleman's clothes?" He shook his head. "I am likely the daftest brother ever to allow you to do this."

"If it were not for your inability to keep money in its proper place rather than in the hands of your friends and any barmaid who will have you, I could spend my days in tea rooms, wearing a proper day dress." Faith crossed her arms and glared at him. "You know as well as I do that, as a lady, to be seen in a coffeehouse conducting business on the behalf of my family would not be spoken of in a favourable fashion. Therefore, I must disguise myself."

"You have twenty thousand pounds, someone would marry you."

Robert *was* perhaps the daftest brother in all of England. He struggled to understand both numbers and her. She did not just want to marry someone whose coffers needed propping up. She wanted a gentleman who knew how to keep both his money and his wife safe and happy.

Her father had been able to almost accomplish such a thing. He had done well in managing his accounts. She knew. She had seen them. And as far as she could tell, her mother had been happy.

However, where her father had failed was in passing on his abilities to his heir. She shook her head. If only she were really a gentleman and not just wearing gentleman's clothing, her father's estate would not be in the state it was now. She understood numbers, and she was far more disciplined than her younger brother about most things in life. However, she was merely a daughter for whom her father had provided handsomely, but to whom he would not leave his fortune.

"What?" Robert asked when Faith only continued to glare at him in silence. "It is true. You have not yet lost your bloom, you are accomplished, and you have a fortune. What else could any Englishman wish for in a wife?"

"You are an idiot," Faith replied. "I should like to be more than a pretty plaything to put on display who funds her husband's enjoyments."

"Must you speak so plainly? It is really not proper."

Faith raised a brow as the carriage rocked as it went around a corner. "I must speak plainly, or you might not understand."

"How many times do I have to apologize for my losses at that card game?"

"And your losses on the horses. And the purchasing of a box at the theatre, which I have yet to sit in for a play. And for leaving me to tend to your friend while you went gallivanting to heaven knows where!" That last part was the most difficult of all her brother's faults to overlook.

"It was a cockfight," he muttered.

She shook her head. Of all the stupid things to do when a friend was injured and ill! It had been a year. She should likely attempt to not yell at him each time she remembered the incident. However, she could not.

Mr. Bertram had come so close to dying! It was fortunate that she had been able to find a way to alert his family to the need to come to collect him. She could not imagine having to lie so near to death with no one to sit watch over her and pray for her recovery.

Oh, she knew Mr. Bertram was as reckless as Robert. That was how Mr. Bertram had sustained his injury and why he had fallen ill. He had not cared for himself as he ought. He had been drinking far too much and spending too many hours chasing pleasure rather than being sensible and sleeping as he should. She shook her head again.

"I just cannot fathom how you could be so heartless," she said to her brother.

"He had fallen. I did not know he would not follow us in a few days."

She rolled her eyes. "You could have waited with him and let the others go on without you."

Robert's head drooped, but he nodded. He looked very much like a penitent child. Drat him! She wanted to stay angry with him. She did not wish to feel like a peevish governess.

"When we have recovered the money you lost, I am certain I will find it easier to forget why I must dress like this and participate in things which, if discovered, would not make me attractive to the proper sort of gentleman – the sort that I wish to secure – one who likes me for me and not just my money."

"So, I am still not to mention your wealth to anyone?"

She shook her head. "I am certain there are those who know it, but I do not need anyone – especially you – broadcasting it far and wide."

"What if you do not succeed this season? Might I then mention it to a few gentlemen of high standing?"

Faith sighed. She was nearly five and twenty. It really was time that she attempted to make a match. It was what was expected, and it was how she would best be able to have a secure future. She pulled her lips back to center from the right where they had puckered. It was not a becoming expression. She must learn to stop making it when thinking about things she would rather not consider.

She could secure her future fortune on her own if she

needed to do so, but she really did need a husband if she were to have children. And she did so love children.

"It is not a gentleman's standing which qualifies or disqualifies him." She sought for how to explain her position to her brother. "Character is more important, Robert. I want an honorable husband who knows how to care for his estate, his wife, and his children's future."

"You want what you are attempting to make me into."

That was it precisely. Faith could not in good conscience allow her brother to be less than the best husband for which a lady could hope. At three and twenty, he was nearing an age when he would begin seriously looking for a Mrs. Eldridge.

Their mother, who understood her easy-going, charming, though not exceptionally thoughtful, son, had entrusted him to Faith before she died. That promise to her mother was what drove Faith to push Robert to be what she knew he could be.

"I wish for you to have a happy marriage." She smiled softly at her brother. "I would not wish for you to be miserable either because you married where you should not – or had to in order to keep the estate in funds – or because you could not care for your family as you wish because the finances are not what they should be." She sighed. "Felicity in marriage really does come down to money, does it not?"

Her brother shook his head. "I do not believe it does."

Faith closed her eyes to keep from rolling them. "In an abstracted fashion, it does. Worry about finances, selling off your inheritance, not being accepted in your usual sphere of friends, or, heaven forbid, being sent to debtors' prison would hamper both a husband's and a wife's contentment and happiness in their union."

"You are far too dramatic, my dear sister. A man and woman can be just as happy on two thousand a year as they can on three."

"If that is where they began," Faith argued. "However, if, for example, your wife is used to having a lady's maid and suddenly has to give up that luxury so that a nursemaid can be acquired for your growing brood, I would think the loss of one to gain the other would cause some strife and unhappiness." She straightened her jacket. "It is only logical, and it is precisely why you must learn to manage your money well."

Robert did not reply. Instead, he turned sullenly toward the window and ignored her for the remainder of their trip. However, as the door to their vehicle was being opened, he lobbed one parting shot.

"I do hope you find a gentleman to love who will cause you to throw caution to the wind. You are too severe. No gentleman wishes to be browbeaten about his accounts."

"Throw caution to the wind, indeed!" Faith stepped out of the carriage and stood beside her brother in front of the coffeehouse. Her heart beat a rapid rhythm in her chest just as it always did before she entered the building. Being discovered would not do her any favours.

"Can we be quick?" she implored.

"Do you wish for a cup of coffee?" Robert asked.

"If it can be brought to Mr. Clarke's room, yes. Otherwise, no. A little faster, please?"

"Trotting into the establishment would draw more eyes than sauntering."

"Can we perhaps not saunter but just walk?" She must have made him excessively irritated with her lecture, for he appeared to be enjoying tormenting her with his nonchalance.

"Oh, very well," he replied with a chuckle. "I shall join you as soon as I have spent a few minutes doing what I do best."

Faith shook her head as she parted from her brother. Talking. Gabbing. Sharing and hearing whatever bit of gossip there was. That is what Robert considered his duty upon entering the coffeehouse. It did not matter to him that other business-minded gentlemen set straight to work.

"Much can be gleaned from a few moments of conversation," she muttered to herself. That was what Robert always said. How much he was gleaning was the issue. He rarely returned to her with any news which was truly useful.

"I would agree."

Faith froze. Her rapidly beating heart leapt into her throat. She had never had to speak to anyone other than Mr. Clarke on the few trips she had made to this establishment. She would box Robert's ears for this later.

"Tom Bertram," the gentleman, who had agreed with her, introduced himself.

Faith swallowed. Mr. Bertram needed no introduction. She knew him – intimately – far more intimately than she knew any other gentleman. Not that he knew that.

"Fa – Fredrick Eldridge." She pitched her voice lower than was normal.

"Eldridge?"

Blast! She should have used a different name. While she was good at numbers, she was not all that adept at lying when caught unawares. If she had been given some warning, she might have been able to concoct a better name and have some clue as to how she might answer anything else Mr. Bertram might ask.

"Yes, yes, Eldridge," she replied as she took a step away from Mr. Bertram and toward Mr. Clarke's door.

"Any relation of Robert Eldridge? I know the possibility might be small, but since Robert is a friend of mine, I thought I would ask." He took a step towards her.

"Oh... uh... well... um... yes, actually, we are related," Faith stammered. "We are cousins. Distant cousins," she added when Mr. Bertram gave her a curious look. Neither she nor Robert had any close cousins as one uncle had never sired children and the other had died before he could even make an attempt at procreating.

"Do you have an appointment with Mr. Clarke?" Mr. Bertram gestured to the door in front of them.

"Yes, we do."

"We?" Tom looked behind him and then turned a full circle. He was mocking her.

"Robert and I," she replied sharply. Her eyes grew wide as she realized she had not pitched her voice lower as she should have done. "I should not keep him waiting. That is Robert's job." She reached for the doorknob, but Mr. Bertram beat her to it.

"It seems *we* is going to include me," he said.

"That cannot be," Faith protested. She and Robert were to meet with Mr. Clarke alone. There were private matters to be discussed, and there was her identity to conceal.

"It is two o'clock, is it not?" Tom took his watch from his pocket and consulted it.

"There must be a mistake."

The door before them opened.

"Ah, good. You are both here," Mr. Clarke said. "I assume your brother will be along soon?" he directed the question to Faith who wished to melt into the floor or vanish, scattered into the air like the smoke from Mr. Clarke's cigar.

Chapter 3

"I thought it a good idea to have the two of you meet," Mr. Clarke continued as he ushered Faith and Tom into his office. "Mr. Bertram needs some advice on how to regain some monies just as your brother is."

"Brother?" Tom couldn't help noticing the way the cheeks of the young gentleman he had met in the hallway had grown brilliantly red, and the fellow seemed to shift uneasily with each mention of that word *brother.* "I thought you said you and Robert were distant cousins."

Mr. Clarke's eyes darted between Tom and young Fredrick. "Did I say something amiss?"

"Yes," Fredrick snapped.

The fellow was not only delicate looking, but he was also easily put out. However, Tom knew for a fact that Fredrick, if that was indeed his name, was not Robert Eldridge's brother. Robert did not have a brother. He had only ever mentioned a sister.

Tom tilted his head and looked carefully at Fredrick. The youngster did bare a remarkable resemblance to

Robert except Robert's neck was not so graceful, nor did Robert have such lovely pink lips and long lashes. If Tom were to be asked to put a wager on it, he would bet that the young gentleman in front of him was not a gentleman at all, but rather a lady in gentlemen's clothing.

"Robert has no brothers," Tom said, breaking the silence in the room.

Mr. Clarke shifted some papers. "Quite right. I had forgotten."

The gentleman had not forgotten a thing. Tom settled back in his chair, waiting and watching until one or the other of the people caught in this falsehood attempted to clear up the *misunderstanding*.

"Well..." Mr. Clarke began but then fell silent.

"You are his friend?" Fredrick asked.

Tom nodded.

"A good friend or the sort who says he is a friend and then tells tales to destroy the other?"

Tom pulled his head back and blinked. "I do not tell tales to destroy anyone. I never have."

"Never?"

Tom shook his head. "Not once. Ever."

"And why are you here?"

"Why should I tell you when I do not even know who you truly are?" Tom replied to the demanding fellow.

"He has spent himself into a precarious position and

wishes to remedy it," Mr. Clarke said. "Much like your... ur... brother."

Mr. Clarke rubbed out his cigar as a clear battle played out in Fredrick's eyes while the young fellow studied Tom.

"Very well." Fredrick, whose voice was no longer low but rather pleasantly womanly, placed a hand on his – or rather, her hat but hesitated. "Not a word of this must leave this room. There are those who would use it to ruin me – not that I can name anyone in particular at this very moment. My friends are quite lovely, but there are others..." She pressed her lips together as if she realized she had been rambling. Her shoulders lifted and lowered as she drew a deliberate breath and took off her hat. "My name is Faith, and Robert is, just as Mr. Clarke has said, my brother."

Beneath that hat was a neatly styled knot of hair the colour of golden sunshine with a few shades of brown and a tinge of a fiery sunset. It was set softly so that some hair would be seen below the brim of her hat just as a gentleman's would be.

"Do you sing?" Tom whispered.

The space between her cobalt blue eyes furrowed.

"I am certain everyone sings, Mr. Bertram."

He pulled his eyes away from her alluring lovely pink lips.

"But not all do it well," he replied.

"Indeed," said Mr. Clarke. "I have not heard Miss Eldridge sing, but I have seen her calculate numbers."

Tom looked at Mr. Clarke and then back to Miss Eldridge. This angelic being was the person who Mr. Clarke thought could help him figure out how to help him with his financial woes? "Mr. Durward said you wished for me to meet someone who might be willing to help me regain my losses."

Mr. Clarke waved a hand in Miss Eldridge's direction. "Miss Eldridge is the best client I have. Her brother's accounts are replenishing themselves quickly."

Tom turned his attention to the lovely lady beside him. He had never imagined that help could come in such a beautiful package. "Will you help me, Miss Eldridge?"

Her eyes grew wide. "Are you not going to utter your shock over my being female and in possession of a brain?"

"Why should I do that?"

That furrow from before once again appeared between her eyes. "Because most gentlemen do."

"Do many know that you are a financial goddess?" Tom smirked as the blush on her cheeks deepened.

"No, but I have been cautioned to keep my intelligence to myself." There was an annoyed edge to her voice.

"Fools. The whole lot of them."

"I do not flirt, Mr. Bertram."

"A pity that," Tom muttered. He would love to flirt with her. "It might surprise you, but I do know that there are ladies who are more cunning than one might expect." He held up a hand. "And not just cunning in how they can claw at each other. But in useful ways."

"Such as finances?"

"I have not met one until now, but I do not disbelieve it possible. How else do many estates operate if the lady of the home does not see to the proper management of the accounts and possessions under her purview?"

That earned him a pleased smile.

"I will not lie. I am impressed with that answer. However, before I give my consent to help you, I must know one thing, Mr. Bertram."

"Anything."

The brow over her left eye rose as if she did not quite believe him. She was a skeptical sort of lady, which made him wonder why she was so distrusting.

"Why do you wish to regain your losses? Is it to keep creditors away from your door so that you are free to come and go and take your ease? Or is it more?"

"I gambled away part of my brother's inheritance."

She remained silent, her eyes searching his.

"I very nearly died due to my reprehensible ways."

"I know," she said softly.

Ah! That must be why she was so distrustful. She had heard about him from her brother. Tom shook his head. How foolish he had been. "I am not that man any longer."

"You are not?" Lashes fluttered over wide, suspicious eyes.

"I have seen the error of my ways. However, I did not pay attention to my father's instruction, and well, I am in need of assistance in learning how to secure my legacy, Miss Eldridge. I would be very grateful if you would help me."

"I will need to consult my brother, of course."

"Of course," Tom replied just as the door opened and allowed the entrance of that brother.

"Close the door," Miss Eldridge snapped at Robert.

"Your coffee," Robert said, placing a cup before her and then turning to close the door. "I had not expected us to have company." He smiled at Tom. "Not that the company is unpleasant. I am, in fact, most pleased to see you, Bertram. How is the leg?"

"It grows stronger. I think I shall be able to rid myself of this soon." Tom lifted his cane.

"Hopefully," Miss Eldridge muttered over her cup of coffee.

"What do you mean hopefully?" Tom asked.

Her eyes grew wide. "Did I say that aloud?"

"Yes, my dear sister, you did."

Miss Eldridge sighed and put her cup of coffee on Mr. Clarke's desk. "Some injuries never heal completely."

"She is being practical," Robert said with a roll of his eyes. "It is one of her most *charming* features."

"Someone in this family ought to be practical."

Tom wanted to chuckle at the look of disdain she leveled at her brother, who merely smiled, causing the look of disdain on his sister's features to deepen. It seemed that these two only resembled each other in features but not temperaments. "Mr. Clarke has suggested I seek help with my finances from your sister."

Robert chuckled and clapped Tom on the shoulder before taking a place leaning against the edge of a small cabinet. "She is good at it. However..."

Tom looked between glaring sister and taunting brother. "I should like to have her help me."

"She is demanding," Robert cautioned.

"I have already discovered that," Tom replied with a grin. "I assure you that I have been thoroughly interrogated as to the sort of friend I am and my purpose in seeking help."

Miss Eldridge gasped and touched each of her fingers on her right hand on the thumb of that hand as if counting as Robert laughed. She gave a further huff.

"I would not call a handful of questions a thorough interrogation."

Her protest caused her brother to laugh harder.

"I cannot just trust my identity to anyone!" she cried in a louder voice. "It is bad enough that I, as a lady of means, am in this establishment, but to be here dressed as I am?" She stood and waved her hand down her person.

Bless Robert for having crossed the room before he infuriated his sister further so that she would have to turn toward him and away from Tom. Her back was as lovely as her front, especially since she was wearing breeches that fit exceptionally well. Not a curve was hidden by that article of clothing. The jacket, that bothersome mass of cloth, was not so obliging in revealing the feminine form beneath it.

"Yes, yes," Robert said, calming some. "I know. You have already lectured me on that in the carriage." He bent to look around his sister. "She is put out with me over my thoughtless extravagances. She does not believe that cockfights and horse races are good uses of funds."

"Because they are not!" Miss Eldridge snapped.

"I was about to agree," Robert retorted. "Why must you always think I am going to disagree with you?"

Miss Eldridge shrugged and unfortunately took a seat. "Because you usually do." Her reply was soft, and to Tom, it seemed as if there was some pain in the admission.

"Only because you drive me to distraction," Robert's reply was soothing. Apparently, he also recognized that his sister was not merely angry. "And before you say it, I know I drive you to distraction as well."

"You do." Her lips curled upward in a small smile.

"But you love me anyway, just as I love you." Robert winked at her.

"It might be too soon to remind me of my love for you."

Robert laughed. "Very well. I shall refrain from saying anything similar until we are in the carriage?"

She shook her head.

"Home?" Robert adjusted.

She shrugged. "That depends on what Mr. Clarke's reports look like." She reached forward and drew a paper towards herself with a "May I?" for Mr. Clarke.

The man readily acceded.

"These are very good numbers," she said after a quick perusal of the paper. "Do you have any investments in mind?" she asked Tom.

He shook his head. "I have been attempting to learn how this all works, and my friend Mr. Durward has suggested some ventures about which he knows."

"Is he conservative?" Her question was asked eagerly as if she were truly interested.

"Excessively."

"And trustworthy? Is he trustworthy?"

Tom smiled. There was no one as trustworthy as his friend Gabriel Durward. "He could not come with me today because he is at home recovering from injuries sustained while proving himself trustworthy to the lady whom he will soon call his wife."

"He is marrying!" Mr. Clarke interjected.

Tom nodded. "He was accepted just this morning."

"He will be wishing to make some changes to his investments, I would assume," Mr. Clark scratched down a note.

"One cannot afford to be too daring when he has a wife to consider." He looked up at Miss Eldridge. "Not that Mr. Durward is daring. He is conservative, but he is aggressive. That might need to be tempered a wee mite."

"He was injured?" Miss Eldridge questioned.

Tom nodded. "He nearly died."

Her lovely blue eyes grew wide.

"It is a long story, but if you were to help me, I am certain we would have the time at some point for me to tell you the tale."

Her eyes sparkled, and her lips pursed, surprising Tom. There was a bit of her teasing brother in her after all. "If I am to help you, I expect to be focused on our task, Mr. Bertram."

"I would have it no other way, but mightn't there be time to have a cup of tea between lectures?"

She smiled. "A cup of coffee or chocolate might be more tempting." She lifted her cup to her lips.

"Whichever you wish."

She closed her eyes as she savoured the sip of coffee she had just taken. Tom swallowed along with her. She was delectably tempting. It was no wonder Robert had never introduced her to any of his friends.

"Will you help me?"

Her eyes opened. "I suppose I shall."

"*We* will call on you tomorrow," Robert said.

Tom nodded his understanding of the raised brow

which accompanied the statement. He would have to attempt to keep his admiration of Robert's sister less obvious. However, he was not entirely certain it was possible.

Chapter 4

Faith and Robert followed the butler up the stairs to the first floor of Mr. Bertram's town house and then down a short hall to a small study just off a drawing room decorated in shades of green and cream. If it would not have been rude, Faith would have stopped at the door to the drawing room and taken in the design. Green was one of her favourite colours. However, as she was not on a tour but rather here on business, she did not stop at the drawing-room door. Instead, she entered the study behind her brother and allowed her eyes to take in its dark wood panelling and fittings.

"Welcome." Mr. Bertram rose from where he sat behind a large desk, which, Faith noticed, was very tidy. There was a lamp on one corner with an inkwell and pen near it, and, to the left, a stack of two books in front of the lamp with a third open book, over which Mr. Bertram must have been poring.

"I was attempting to decide where we should begin." He pulled one of the chairs that stood in front of the desk around and behind the piece of furniture so that it was next to his and to his right. "Miss Eldridge." He motioned to his large leather chair.

"You wish for me to sit there?" In his seat? Where the master of the house should sit? It seemed wrong.

"You are the teacher," he said with one of his charming smiles that caused her to want to sigh.

She lifted her chin and scolded herself. She was not here to admire Mr. Bertram. "I could sit on –" Or perhaps, not. Tom had dropped into the chair he had just placed behind his desk.

"I insist." He motioned once more to his large leather chair. "Will you be joining us, Eldridge? Or would you rather take your ease in the drawing room?"

It was then, as she was just about to take her place at the desk, that Faith noticed the door which led from the study to the green drawing room they had passed. "May I look at it?"

"The drawing room?" Tom asked in surprise.

Faith nodded. "I know it is forward to ask. However, we passed it on our way here, and the glimpse I got of it was so lovely. Oh, no! You do not need to rise," she added as Tom reached for his cane. "I will just peek in the door to satisfy my curiosity."

Tom waved his hand toward the door. "We can take some tea in there later if you wish. I was just going to have it brought in here, but the drawing room would be more comfortable."

"There is even a table for it," Faith replied, turning back toward Mr. Bertram. "It would be perfect. It is very well decorated," she added as she returned to that formidable chair behind the desk.

"I cannot take credit for any of that. I believe my mother was the one who chose the décor."

"You do not know?" How did one not know if one's mother had or had not decorated a room? Faith knew precisely which pieces had been placed where by her mother and what fittings had been purchased by whom and when.

Tom shook his head. "I do not."

"How?" Faith flopped back in her chair.

Robert chuckled. "Gentlemen are not so interested in paint and fabric as you are, Faith." He had taken a book from one of the shelves that lined the wall behind the desk and was making his way to a chair in a small alcove which looked absolutely perfect for curling up in for a long read.

"But surely Mr. Bertram would have noticed some activity. Decorating or, more likely redecorating, causes a fair bit of disturbance."

"If he were not here when it was done, then he might not notice," Robert argued.

Faith scowled at her brother before turning to Mr. Bertram. "Were you here when it was being decorated?"

Tom shook his head. "For me, it has always looked as it

does now save for a few pieces that have been shifted or a new painting that was hung or the like." He was smiling as he watched her.

She blushed. "Well, that is acceptable then."

"I am glad to hear it."

"Tell me what this ledger is." She would much rather his eyes be on his books than on her. She did not enjoy the prickly feeling it sent up her spine. It was not at all comfortable or conducive to wishing to add up sums and consider percents.

Mr. Bertram shifted closer to her so that he could see the book which lay open on the desk. The action did not make that distracting tingling sensation go away. If anything, it made it worse. She gave herself a mental shake and pulled her mind away from the handsome gentleman beside her – or, at least, she tried to. He was, after all, going to remain at her side, and she must converse with him. Ignoring him would not do. She must just ignore how attractive he was.

"This is the book that shows the amount of my brother's inheritance which was lost – no, not lost," Mr. Bertram corrected, "squandered."

There was a bitter edge to his words that tugged at Faith's heart. It seemed he was truly repentant for having wasted his funds. She had heard that same tone in Robert's voice when trying to reconcile accounts.

"And the other books?"

"Those are household accounts. I thought I should have them at the ready in case you suggested retrenching."

She tipped her head and studied the covers of the closed books. He was not only repentant but also determined to recoup his losses. Retrenching was not something that came easily for many. "Have you done any retrenching already?" she asked. "It is an excellent way to earn money without risk."

"I stay home more often than is my normal wont and have not purchased any new suits of clothes since the season began."

"That is commendable." She peeked at her brother, who seemed to sense her look and shifted uncomfortably. "Doing without a few items now will make for a brighter future. Oh, my! That is a substantial amount, is it not?" She queried after having taken a look at the book before her.

"It is," Tom agreed as he pulled two sheets of paper out from under the household account books on the desk. "This is a list of investments my father has made and over which he has given me control."

Faith scanned the items. "These seem very good. I am not certain they could be made much better without posing too much risk." She shook her head. "You cannot afford to take too great a risk with this much of a debt that needs repayment, for you do not wish for it to grow. Do you have any additional funds that are not already invested? Something that would cause little inconvenience if lost or diminished?"

Tom pulled the bottom page from her hands and pointed at a figure. "That is money which is liquid." He smiled sheepishly at her. "I sold a few things, and there was some money that my father was able to give me for this venture. He is quite happy that I am finally attempting to take responsibility for Mansfield and its holdings."

"You sold things to do this?" That was a very noble gesture. Again, she peeked at her brother.

"I did."

"I think I will have an easier time of reading in the drawing room," Robert said, pushing up from his place. "There is too much talking and too many pointed glares in here."

Tom chuckled. "I take it that your brother has not yet come to the point of retrenching?"

Faith shook her head and smiled. "He has not, but I have."

"You?" Mr. Bertram's asked incredulously. "But is it not your brother's doing which has caused his troubles?"

"Yes." Faith sighed. "However, if I wish for my money to still be intact when it is needed, it is best if I forego a dress or a pair of slippers on occasion." She lowered her voice. "Robert goes without a few things as well. He just does not know it."

Again, Tom chuckled. "Such as?"

"Our cook is excellent, and so is Robert's valet. Both

can create the appearance of finery with a little less than some might need."

"And your brother has no idea you are doing this?"

"To be fair, I did tell him that if he did not find a way to retrench on his own, I would assist him."

"But he has no idea you are assisting?"

Faith shrugged. "Not yet. I suppose when we review the accounts next week, I will be forced to admit to some of it. However, I hope that by being slightly devious, I can show him that retrenching is not as difficult or painful as he might think it is going to be. The thought of doing without something to which you have grown accustomed can be a frightening thing."

And it smacked of failure. She knew that Robert felt as if he had failed. He did not say it, but she could see it in his features when she refused to go shopping as he suggested or declined an invitation to some soiree that might require a small expenditure of money.

"We are not destitute or anywhere near it," she added. "I am just cautious, and one day, I assume he will marry."

"A family is a heavy responsibility," Tom agreed softly.

"Do not tell him I said anything. He would be embarrassed."

Tom shook his head. "I would not dream of embarrassing him. He has been a good friend." He paused and looked away toward the drawing room and then back at her. "I must ask you a question regarding him."

Tom looked again at the drawing-room door. "I am attempting to change my ways –"

"As is Robert – even if he is not doing so as willingly as I would wish. Father's death." She sighed and then drew a breath. It had been a year, and yet it was difficult to speak of it.

"I understand."

Faith looked up from studying her hands.

"I nearly died." He covered her clasped hands with his. "Death is a good soberer of the self-indulgent. I am sorry that your father died."

Faith pulled one hand free from his and brushed a wayward tear from her cheek. "I suppose we should discuss what sorts of investments might interest you."

"An excellent idea." With a questioning look, he withdrew his hand from covering hers.

"Thank you," Faith whispered. "For understanding and your condolences. I just cannot speak about it."

The replying smile he gave her before taking another sheet of paper out of his desk was understanding. It was enough to make her wish to sigh again. She pulled herself straight and accepted the paper he handed her.

"I would like to begin with this," he said. "My friend, Mr. Durward, is looking for partners."

Chapter 5

Two days later, Tom settled into a chair in Gabe's study. The surgeon and Gabe's mother could confine Gabe to his house, but they were unable to keep him from work. Tom knew that if his friend had his way, Gabe would be at the warehouse watching over the things that still were part of his business there. However, that warehouse was a business which was not going to remain a part of Gabe's life.

Things were changing. Gabe would soon have a wife and, after that, likely children. Added to those changes was the fact that Gabe preferred to be his own man and work with integrity, which was something he did not feel was entirely possible in his current situation.

"What has our friend's face so twisted?" Tom whispered to Mr. Waller who was sitting silently in front of Gabe's desk.

"My face is not twisted," Gabe said without lifting his eyes from his papers. "I am making a few last calculations about my future." He lifted his eyes to look at Tom. "Or rather, *our* future?" he asked hopefully.

Tom shrugged. "My financial advisor seems to think your scheme is worthy of my funds as long as they are funds which can be lost without further damaging my estate."

With a pleased smile, Gabe returned his attention to his papers.

"A conservative fellow, is he?" Waller asked.

The image of deep blue eyes, sunset blonde hair, and pleasant curves caused Tom to smile as he shook his head. "Conservative, yes. A fellow, no."

Gabe's head popped up from his work. "The expert Clarke mentioned is female?"

"Very."

Temptingly female. Distractingly female. Female enough for Tom to wish he had not declared his old self a thing of the past for he would dearly love to steal a kiss or more from Miss Eldridge. However, he *had* declared his old self gone, and with it, he had packed away his old actions. Therefore, he would have to endure the alluring femininity of his tutor and refrain from pressing matters any further than friendship – and a possible dance or two at a ball, should they ever meet at such an event.

He tipped his head and looked past Gabe. He could, perhaps, offer to take her for a drive through the park. They could discuss business while driving as easily as they could in a study or drawing room – as they had done yesterday at the Eldridge's home.

He brought his focus back to his companions when Waller nudged his arm. Both Waller and Gabe were looking at him as if he should have some sort of response for them. For the life of him, he had no idea what they had asked. He had not even been aware that they were speaking. Miss Eldridge was a distraction even when she was not present.

"I apologize; I was woolgathering." His ears burned at the admission.

"That is answer enough," Waller said with a laugh.

"Waller wished to know if this female advisor was attractive," Gabe explained.

Tom sighed. "Her intelligence does not outshine her beauty, and she is not short of intelligence."

"I will assume she is unattached?"

"I can admire the beauty of a lady even if she is married without falling prey to desire," Tom grumbled in response to the stern look that had accompanied Gabe's question.

"I should hope you can resist falling prey to desire even is she is *not* married," Gabe added. "However, falling for her charms and acquiring a wife would not be a bad thing."

Tom laughed at the uncharacteristic sigh which followed his friend's word. Gabe was utterly besotted with his betrothed.

"When I am certain I have established a good path to financial recovery," Tom said, "I will begin contemplating a wife. Until then, I shall just admire the flowers in the garden."

"Unless the thorns from one of those roses snag your sleeve and refuse to let it go," said Durward.

"My heart is not yet in danger," Tom assured his friend and himself. Miss Eldridge was becoming a good friend, and Tom found her tempting. However, that was the extent of his interest. "Speaking of thorny beauties, how is Miss Crawford?"

"A beauty she is. However, I will not agree that she is thorny."

"And yet she has snagged you," Tom replied.

Again, Gabriel Durward, the most business-minded man Tom had the pleasure of calling friend, sighed like a hopelessly lost fool.

"That she has. That she has," he agreed. "She was well when I saw her yesterday, and if she remains well, I shall get to see her later today, for she and the Grants are to come to dinner."

Still wearing a smitten grin, Gabe applied himself to his work, writing one final note on his page before putting his pen in its holder. "Since I am still confined to my home, Waller was scouting some locations for a warehouse yesterday."

Waller was to be the third man in their undertaking. He had a little money and a fair bit of experience when it came to knowing goods and how to acquire them. He had been paying close attention to details on each and every voyage he had taken, whether it was on a privateer or a regular ship.

To Tom, Waller seemed a good fit. Of course, the fact that he had earned Gabe's approval was enough for Tom to accept the man despite any skills or lack thereof.

"However," Gabe continued, "as soon as I am allowed out of my door, I intend to call upon Mr. Gardiner. If there is anyone who can provide advice for us in this venture, Gardiner is our man."

He paused, his brow furrowing as he looked at Tom. It appeared as if he were not entirely confident how Tom was going to react to what he had to say. No doubt, he was considering how to counter any opposition. "I have also been considering adding a storefront to our venture."

The idea was not without merit. But then, Tom did not expect Gabe to present him with an idea which was anything less than profitable. "That would increase profit, would it not?"

Gabe nodded slowly. "Indeed, it would since I would be both the supplier and the shopkeeper – not that I would actually keep the shop. We would need to hire someone to see to the running of the day to day workings of the business. Do you think your advisor would still approve of your participation in this venture if we were to add a store to the equation?"

"I cannot see why she would not. I am using funds that will not harm my estate any further."

"You would still only be an investor and would not need to soil your hands," Gabe added. "It would all be very respectable. We must remember your station."

All this was said in a flat, matter-of-fact fashion just as Gabe always spoke. He was not one to cover up the possible conflicts, he would, instead, find a solution – often, before any objection could be raised. Tom figured that such a skill was what made Gabe such a good businessman.

Gabe folded the paper upon which he had been writing and handed it to Tom. "I have listed the few changes we are now discussing on this page."

Tom chuckled. "You knew I would agree before you even asked?"

"He would have given you no choice," Waller replied. "Durward usually gets what he wishes."

"One way or another," Gabe added with a grin.

Tom slipped the paper into his pocket. He knew his friend was not opposed to making his point forcefully known.

"My first venture into an investment that does not involve a set of cards or dice." Tom patted his pocket.

"But just as much of a gamble," Waller cautioned.

"Ah, but I am not playing with gentlemen who wish to leave me with empty pockets," Tom returned.

Gabe pushed up from his chair and propped a crutch under the arm Tom knew had not been damaged in reclaiming his ship and rescuing Miss Crawford. "Mother insists that you have tea before you leave." He pointed at first Waller and then Tom. "Both of you. You have joined our family, it seems, whether you wish it or not."

A short time later, Tom mounted his horse and began his journey homeward.

The few minutes Tom had passed having tea with Mrs. Durward, Waller, and Gabe had been pleasant, as they normally were. Tom found he did not mind being part of Gabe's family. Mrs. Durward was a far more attentive mother than his mother had ever been.

Tom's mother had loved him and doted on him, but her nerves always seemed to get the better of her. When they did, she would either become fidgety and unable to focus on what needed attention, or she ignored the source of agitation. Reprimanding a child was most certainly a thing that agitated his mother's nerves, and so she rarely did much more than caution that such a thing was not good.

However, where his mother was indolent, his father was stern.

At a young age, Tom had learned to behave according to which parent was at home. Such shifting had followed him into adulthood. It was how he managed to escape many potentially damaging escapades. One did not wish for his behaviour to be published far and wide when that behavior might fall on the ears of a demanding father. Some misbehaviour could be tolerated, but Tom's father's patience had a limit.

Tom had found himself on the wrong side of his father's limit on more than one occasion. It had never been a pleasant lecture which followed. It was a wonder he still cared for his younger brother at all as Edmund was always being held up as the more exemplary of the two sons. Bitterness over such a thing was what made it easy to squander his brother's inheritance. It had been foolish to do so. He knew that now as he looked at life differently, having been so near the end of it as he had been.

Tom drew his horse to a stop. "Miss Eldridge?" He had not expected to see her in this section of town. Nor had he expected to see her dressed more like a maid than the lady of quality he knew her to be. However, she had been dressed as a gentleman when he first met her. So it really should not surprise him so much as it did, he supposed.

"Mr. Bertram." Miss Eldridge dipped a shallow curtsey.

"You are far from home." He slid down from his horse.

"Indeed, I am. As are you."

Apparently, she did not wish to tell him why she was here. He could see it in how she shifted and would not meet his eyes.

"I was calling on Mr. Durward. He hopes to add something to our venture."

That caught her attention and stopped her from looking anxiously up and down the street.

"He hopes to add a storefront."

Her brow furrowed while her lovely lips pinched together.

"Does the investment still meet your approval?"

She sighed. "So many do not pay their bills."

She said it so softly that Tom was not sure if she was talking to herself or had meant to include him in her thoughts.

"But the profit margin is higher."

She shook her head. "There are employees to pay."

"There are employees in a warehouse as well, and a merchant might not make good on his promise to pay."

She blew out a breath. "It is your money."

"But do you approve?" Tom was not certain why he felt such a compulsion to hear her say she approved of his decision to be part of this venture. It was likely because she understood numbers better than he did.

She shrugged. It was not the vote of confidence for which he had hoped.

"I will give it a bit more thought, but I suppose there is no more risk in it now than there was before." She shook her head. "No, no. I do not need to think any longer. It is a fine idea. Should you lose part or all of the money you are using, it will not harm your estate." She pulled her lower lip between her teeth as her brow furrowed again. "Although it will not help it either," she added.

"I trust Mr. Durward."

She smiled at him. "Of course, you do. I should have considered that. You can tell me the particulars when next we speak, but I must be going." She dipped another small curtsey and then scurried away.

Tom watched with curiosity as she stopped at a house and knocked on the door before opening the door for herself and entering.

Chapter 6

"Good day, Mrs. Johns," Faith greet the lady who was sitting near the window, stitching a petticoat. "How are you feeling today?" She placed her bonnet on the table near the fireplace and draped her pelisse over a chair next to the table.

"I am doing quite well today." Mrs. Johns lifted her hand and wiggled her fingers. "Not even a small ache yet."

"Then you are healing well." Faith searched the workbasket for a thimble, needle, and thread.

"I believe I am," the lady replied.

Faith enjoyed these moments with her friend's mother even if it did require her to dress in a drab costume so that it was easier to traverse the streets in this part of town without being thought of as a lady of much means.

"And your foot? Have the soaks helped the sores?"

"Immensely, but I must still hobble about with that crutch you gave me. It hurts far too much to walk on it without that." She tipped her head toward the wooden crutch leaning against the wall behind her chair.

To Faith, Mrs. Johns looked well. The brown curls that were not covered by her frilly black cap framed a smiling face. Smiles from Mrs. Johns were few and far between in the past few months, but not without good reason.

"And your heart?" Faith posed the question in a whisper as she took a seat in the second chair in front of the window.

"It aches, but not as it did. I believe it is also healing each day." She sighed and looked around the room. "I am even beginning to think of this as home."

"That is good."

Faith threaded her needle and began stitching a seam on a pair of men's small clothes. It was not a glamorous way to provide assistance to her friend's mother, but it was a useful way to do it. She bit the inside of her cheek to keep from smiling. Robert would not be pleased to know she was sewing such an intimate article of clothing for a gentleman to whom she was not related.

The sound of a piano being played while someone sang drifted across the hall and into the sitting room.

"Olivia has a new student," Mrs. Johns said. "That makes three."

"I am glad to hear it. Nobody sings as sweetly as Olivia," Faith replied with a smile. "Those young ladies are fortunate to have such a good teacher."

"You sing just as sweetly."

"Thank you."

Faith applied herself to keeping her stitches close and tidy, but after a few moments, she could not help but hum along with the tune being taught in the music room.

It was not an actual music room. It had been designed as a dining room, but when Olivia and her mother had moved into this small terraced house, it had presented the best prospect for a classroom. It was close to the door and had a window which faced the street and gave a good source of light so that a lamp did not always need to be lit. The savings of a few pence here and there were important for two ladies left with little to their name and in such an unexpected fashion.

Mr. Johns had been killed in the very accident in which Mrs. Johns sustained her injuries. Unfortunately, Mr. Johns had not been adept at keeping his finances in as lovely a state as his wardrobe, and the new heir – some long-lost cousin – was not keen on paying for the upkeep of two ladies beyond seeing to the rental of this house for them.

Thankfully, Mrs. Johns and Olivia had been provided for in a small way in Mr. John's will. Still, it was not enough to keep either his wife or daughter from having to take up some form of work to ensure they had food, clothing, and warmth.

Faith jabbed her needle into the fabric she held. Men, who did not know how to see to their accounts and manage money appropriately, were in danger of leaving those they held dear to scratch their way through life once they were gone. This tableau – right here, in this small sitting room where Mrs. Johns was stitching clothing for some family to make a few shillings while her daughter earned a few more by offering lessons — was what she wished Robert would take to heart. Gentlemen were responsible for their loved ones even after death – and he, up until now, had been the furthest thing from responsible.

However, Faith would not suffer this fate should her brother be taken from her tomorrow, for she had seen to her own security. She had her dowry and that which she had managed to earn by investing her allowance with Mr. Clarke.

"Did your maid attend you?" Mrs. Johns asked.

"She did. I believe she was hoping to air out your room today."

Mrs. Johns shook her head. "It is not right," she muttered.

"Not right for me to see to the care of an injured friend?"

Mrs. Johns peeked up from her work. "You know of what I speak."

She did. Faith knew that the significant lowering of circumstance – from a fine estate to – she looked around the small room – this — was perhaps the most challenging part of Mrs. Johns' injuries.

"But it is beginning to feel like home?"

Mrs. Johns nodded. "Strangely, yes."

"As soon as you no longer need that crutch," Faith said hopefully, "you will be able to move about and do all the things you wish to do that would make this house feel even more like home. My maid and I are no substitutes for your talents. Do you remember when it snowed that one winter when I was visiting, and Olivia and I were unable to go to the village to gather all the things we thought we needed for a party?"

The lady across from her smiled. "Such pouting!"

"We were not very happy," Faith laughed. "But you knew just how to make the few things we had available look like the finest decorations in any drawing room in town."

"I am certain it was not that well done," Mrs. Johns replied with a laugh.

"Why Faith! You have performed a miracle." Olivia Johns, tall, slender, and beautiful, breezed into the room. "I have not heard Mama laugh in so very long." She stopped to kiss Faith's cheek and then her mother's before collecting some sewing on which to work.

"We were reminiscing about that party we had one winter," Faith explained. "I am eager to see how your mother will improve this place once she is able to move about freely."

"It will not be long," Olivia said. "She was limping across her room last night." She peered up from preparing to work and gave her mother a pointed look. "Not that she should have been, but she managed it."

Faith watched as Mrs. Johns merely raised an eyebrow at her daughter but seemed unmoved by the gentle scold.

"I hear you have a new student," Faith said, turning back to Olivia.

"She is so promising. Did you hear her just now? Not quite the voice of an angel such as you have, but very pleasant."

"An angel? Me?" Faith shook her head and laughed.

"You are too modest," Olivia chided. "There was an exceptionally handsome gentleman who paused outside my window just after you arrived," she added.

Faith's needle stilled. Had Mr. Bertram followed her?

"Indeed?" She tried to keep her voice even so as not to give away how excessively curious she was. "What did he look like?"

"He was riding a bay and wearing a dark blue great coat. His features were sharp – not rounded – angular, and his hair was brown. I could have looked at him for hours if he had stayed in front of my window, and if I had not had a student who deserved my attention."

"He most certainly sounds attractive." Apparently, Mr. Bertram had followed her. She would dearly like to know why. "Do you think he was listening to your music?"

Olivia shook her head and laughed. "I should hope not from the puzzled expression on his face."

The room fell into silence for three ticks of the clock on the table in the corner.

"Do you know him?" Olivia asked.

"I believe I might." Faith tied off her thread and snipped it. She needed a fresh length to complete the next seam.

"Well, out with it!" Mrs. Johns cried. "I have heard no talk of handsome men in this age. The two of you used to speak of them so often." There was a wistfulness in her tone.

Olivia, of course, could not attend soirees in town. There was not enough money for such things, and even if there were enough funds to allow for a ballgown and slippers, she was still in mourning for her father, though she had begun to wear lavenders.

"Do you recall that I have been helping Robert with his finances?"

Both ladies nodded.

"And that we sometimes frequent a coffeehouse so that I might speak with a stockbroker?"

Again, they nodded.

"Well, on our last visit to that coffeehouse, there was a gentleman there whom the stockbroker thought could benefit from my assistance."

Olivia's eyes were wide. "You met *that* gentleman at the coffeehouse?"

"Yes."

"While you were dressed as..."

"Yes, while I was wearing breeches and a jacket."

"Oh, my!"

"Indeed," Faith agreed with her friend.

"Does he know you are not a gentleman?" Mrs. Johns asked.

Faith sighed. "Yes. He happens to be a friend of my brother."

"Him?" Olivia pointed toward the street.

Faith looked, but there was no one there. "Yes."

Though there was no one from whom she needed to keep a secret in the house, she leaned forward and lowered her voice. "Mr. Bertram, the gentleman on the horse in front of your window, is the friend who fell from a horse and stayed at our estate for a time."

Olivia's mouth dropped open.

"The one you cared for?" asked Mrs. Johns.

Faith nodded. "So, he has seen me improperly dressed, and I have seen him..."

"Even less properly dressed," Mrs. Johns supplied.

"Does... Does... does he know?" Once again, Olivia waved her hand at the window.

"I do not believe he does." Faith was thankful for that. Although after meeting him today, she was a trifle worried that her secret might not remain a secret. "He barely saw anything of me. He was not in his right senses – floating between wakefulness and sleep. And, remember, I dressed as a maid while I tended to him. But then, someone had to see to his care."

She had dressed as a maid to make it more challenging for him to identify her if he should recall her help. It was not appropriate for a gently bred young woman to sit alone with a gentleman in his bedchamber for days. Nor was it appropriate for such a young woman to help tend to his needs alongside his man. However, as a maid in an understaffed home, she could push the bounds of propriety much further without it becoming a great item of gossip.

"My brother was gone when I arrived to find a feverish stranger languishing in a barely staffed house because Robert had not intended to be in residence and had not bothered to inform anyone of his arrival." She placed her work in her lap and stared out the window. "I still do not understand how anyone can leave his injured friend behind to go make merry." She shook her head. "Mr. Bertram is very nice. He does not even seem to be upset with Robert for having left him. They greeted each other as if nothing so dire as nearly dying had ever occurred. Men are very odd creatures."

Mrs. Johns chuckled. "They are indeed, but then they would say the same about us."

"You are likely right. Robert seems incapable of understanding me."

"You are not an easily understood lady," Olivia said.

"Most ladies do not dress as men and go visit stockbrokers, nor do they dress as maids to attend to sick friends." She shook her head. "How did you not die of mortification upon meeting him? If I had seen a gentleman in nothing but his small clothes, I am sure I could not even meet his eyes whether he knew I had seen him or not."

Faith's cheeks flushed. "It was much easier to keep my eyes on his face rather than risk remembering what is hidden beneath his jacket and trousers."

Mrs. Johns laughed. "Oh, Faith. You are such good medicine to my soul." She continued to laugh until she had to seek her handkerchief to dry the corner of her eyes.

"I do hope he does not remember seeing me in this dress." She should have worn her longer pelisse, but that one was too nice to be wearing in this part of town when one was pretending to be a maid and not a lady of means.

"You mean he saw you today?"

Faith nodded. "I tried to escape as quickly as I could, but he had a question regarding an investment. I do not know why it could not wait until next time we meet, but it seemed important that he have his answer now and not later."

Mrs. Johns was laughing again. "What other lady attempts to escape from a handsome gentleman? Oh, Faith, you are a treasure."

"A lady, who wishes for the gentleman to not recognize her pretending to be a maid just as she did when he was ill at her brother's estate, and who slept in the chair beside him to keep watch over his fever will try to avoid discovery."

She had been so scared that he was going to die before the apothecary could come on that first night, and then later, she had been equally as worried that his family would not arrive to see him before he succumbed. She could still feel his hand in hers. His grip would tighten at times as he coughed and groaned, and she would sing to him just as her mother used to sing to her.

"I should not tease," Mrs. Johns apologized.

"No, no," Faith assured her with a smile, "I am unusual. I know this. But I truly do hope he did not recognize me, or our meeting tomorrow could be very awkward."

Chapter 7

Tom stood in front of a very grand and familiar building, looking at its door. He had not been inside this particular establishment since before his accident. It was a place of great pleasure – drink, cards, friends – but it was also a bastion of his former life.

"Are you going in?"

Tom shook his head as he greeted Charles Edwards, who had approached him. "Are you?"

He did not know Edwards as well as he knew some gentlemen, but he had played a few games with the man and had entered into more than one bet with him. However, that was before the miraculous transformation of Mr. Edwards from rake to respectable gentleman.

"Only to meet Crawford and Linton." Edwards nodded toward the door. "Join me."

Tom looked toward the entrance to his club. Could he enter and exit without falling prey to that which he wished to avoid? After a moment of careful contemplation, while Mr. Edwards waited patiently, Tom decided there was only one way to discover the answer. "Very well, I shall join you."

"Excellent. I have heard from Crawford, through his sister, that you are bent on becoming one of us." Edwards lowered his voice as if imparting a secret of great importance. "Respectable."

Tom chuckled. "I am attempting it, yes."

Edwards handed his hat and coat to the servant standing near the door and waited for Tom to do the same. "I also heard you were injured in a riding accident." He nodded toward Tom's cane.

"I stupidly thought I could take a fence, but I was wrong."

"Port, whisky, or brandy?"

Tom's brow furrowed at the odd question.

"I assume you were well into your cups to misjudge a fence. You are a friend of Eldridge, are you not?"

"I am," Tom replied as Edwards led him to a table where Henry Crawford and Trefor Linton sat.

"Eldridge's horses are some of the best around, and any of his friends, I would assume, know their animals well — meaning, you are no novice rider. Therefore, to misjudge a jump was the result of too much libation. I would bet a pound I am right. However, I have had my fill of bets for some time."

Tom chuckled. He had heard about the bet Edwards had placed declaring he could steal a kiss from the lady who was now his betrothed. The bet had almost cost him his happiness with the lady. Anyone who had come so close to losing something of great value often amended their ways to avoid such a thing happening again.

"Whisky," Tom said as he took a seat and greeted each of the others. "It nearly cost me my life, so the cane, though bothersome, in comparison, it is not so bad a thing."

"Finely spoken," Linton commended. "A dissipated life will never lead to anything good."

"On that you are wrong. It led me to a wonderful young lady," Edwards retorted.

"Whom you nearly lost," Linton grumbled.

"True, but had I not made that bet, and had I not had a reputation which caused you to attack me over some rumor, and..." He held up a finger to mark his point. "If Crawford had not lost his heart and sought to amend his ways which led to my being required to help your sister protect his reputation, I might not ever have met my future Mrs. Edwards. Therefore, a dissipated life – no, no, two dissipated lives have led me to my current blissful state and to Crawford being just as happily tied to your sister."

"I maintain that your dissipation did you no favours," Linton protested.

"I am happily betrothed, and you are not," Edwards said pointedly. "I think it is your lack of dissipation which hinders you from finding happiness, my friend."

Tom was not certain how Charles Edwards and Trefor Linton could be such good friends. One was a renown rake not unfamiliar with scandal, and the other was the sort of gentleman whose name was never even thought of in relation to a scandal.

"I am not ready to be married," Linton retorted.

"I am nearly certain Mr. Bertram did not join us to hear you two argue about foolishness," Henry interjected.

"Apologies," Linton said.

"Oh, I had no particular reason for joining you other than Edwards offered." Tom nodded his thanks for the glass of port which was placed before him.

"Bertram?"

"Eldridge," Tom replied, replacing his glass on the table without so much as taking a sip before turning toward his friend.

"May I?" Robert asked, motioning to a chair.

"Of course," Edwards replied.

Tom suspected that if they could fit twenty chairs at this table, Edwards was the sort to fill them all and look to squeeze in a few extra.

"Do not tell Faith, I was here," he whispered as he sat down. "She will say it was an unnecessary expense." He looked at the other fellows. "Have you all met my sister?"

"Two of us are betrothed," Edwards said. "But Linton here is looking for a wife."

"I just said I was not," Linton snapped. "Not that your

sister is not worth considering, Eldridge," he added quickly. "I have met her. Last year at a musicale, if I remember correctly."

"I was not asking for that reason," Robert said with a laugh.

"Does she play an instrument?" Tom asked.

"You do not know?" Edwards asked in surprise.

Tom shook his head. "Eldridge refused to introduce me to his sister until recently." It was not precisely a formal introduction which he had received in Mr. Clarke's office – more of a forced confession – but the others did not need to know that.

"I can understand that," Linton muttered.

"As can I," Tom agreed. "I would like to say I would not wish to introduce such a person as I was to my sisters, but I did. Therefore, I cannot claim to not do what I did." He held up a hand. "I am not condemning anyone but myself with such a statement. I was not the brother my sisters needed."

He would likely regret that all his life. Julia seemed happy enough with her husband, but Maria – well, perhaps one day he would be able to do something for her. However, first, he needed to get his financial affairs in order. Then, he might be able to convince his father that Maria could be accepted back into the family – at least, for a visit.

"Does your sister play an instrument?" Tom asked Robert once again.

"The piano," Robert replied.

"She did not play the piano at that musicale," Linton inserted. "She sang. I only remember because her voice is among the prettiest voices I have heard."

"She does sing like an angel," Robert admitted.

Tom's eyebrows rose.

"And she is as pretty as her voice," Robert muttered. "However, there is a touch of fire in her tongue – at least, there is for me. Not that I can blame her. I have been careless. But no more. I must mend my ways now that my inheritance has fallen to me."

The table fell silent.

"It is not easy to come into one's inheritance," Linton admitted.

"Indeed, it is not," Henry agreed. "I did not step into it gracefully. I fought it and ignored it for some time. However, thanks to Linton and his sister, I am finally settling into it."

"I am attempting to tend to mine now before my father passes it on to me," Tom admitted as he swirled the contents of his glass. The right side of his mouth curled up as he considered the pretty lady who was assisting him. If all his teachers had been as beautiful as Miss Eldridge, he would have applied himself better to his studies.

"If you need help," Linton offered, raising his glass in a small salute to Tom.

"Eldridge is helping me at present as is Durward, but I thank you for your offer."

"Durward is the gentleman who is marrying Crawford's sister, is he not?" Linton asked.

"Yes," Tom answered.

"And Eldridge is helping you as well?" There was a hint of skepticism in the man's tone.

"My sister is," Robert answered in a whisper, "but no one is to know that." He gave each of his companions a pointed glare. "She lectures enough now. I do not wish for any further diatribes. Ladies with too much knowledge are not sought after and all that." He waved his hand in the air and then, blew out a breath. "And I would not wish to harm her chances. She deserves to find a good match."

Tom could hear the love Robert had for his sister in his tone as he spoke, but then, Robert had always spoken well of her. That coupled with the way he had steadfastly refused to introduce her to any of his reprobate friends spoke loudly to how much he adored her.

"You may wish to send Bertram to me," Linton said, placing his empty glass on the table and moving to rise. "My sister was allowed to help Crawford and look where that led." Linton grinned in opposition to his words. "I must say she did an excellent job of improving him."

"Indeed, she did," Henry said.

"There is nothing to fear," Tom assured them. "I do not intend to even entertain the idea of looking for a wife until I have my finances in order."

Linton snorted in disbelief.

"Truly," Tom replied.

"Well, I wish you well," Linton answered.

"Would you like to join us?" Edwards said as he rose. "We are going to serve some soup to the less fortunate."

To Tom, it appeared as if only Edwards was excited about the prospect before them. "No, thank you."

"Will you come with me?" Robert asked as the other gentlemen left. "I had thought to go home and find some way to amuse myself since Faith would not accept the invitation to the Howard's soiree this evening."

"She only wishes for you to save the expense." Tom rose to follow his friend. He would much rather follow Robert home and spend a few hours playing billiard or cards with a friend than returning to his own home to spend a boring evening reviewing accounts before tomorrow's meeting and then, eventually, reading until he grew weary enough to retire to his bed for some sleep.

"I know, but how is she to find a husband if she stays at home?"

"I am surprised she has not found one already." Although part of Tom was glad she had not.

"She has exacting standards." Robert shook his head. "I

fear she has concocted some impossible image in her head and will never be truly satisfied."

"I am certain you fear for nothing. She is sensible. Surely, her aspirations are not unattainable." She would likely be too sensible to ever consider him. He glanced surreptitiously at this friend. Robert was not looking his direction. There was no chance he had seen Tom's startled and unhappy expression at the thought of Miss Eldridge never considering him.

Robert sighed. "Perhaps. Although it is Faith, and she can be unmovable at times."

The two friends mounted their horses and began their journey to the Eldridge's home.

"Truth be told. I fear she is putting off attempting to find a match until she has seen me improved enough to be considered worthy of a wife." Robert sighed again but did not go on.

Tom suspected there was more that Robert wished to say, but he would not press his friend on the matter. Sometimes there were things which weighed heavily on a person's heart but were not able to be put into words for just anyone – even a good friend. Was that not why Tom rarely spoke of his father's approval — or rather the lack of his father's approval — and why he never spoke of his mother's sadness? As contrary as it would sound to many who considered a gentleman to be made of strong, stern stuff, the male heart which lay beneath the bluster and boasting was a fragile thing.

Chapter 8

"Everything seems to be in order," Mr. Clarke peered up from the papers which lay before him.

Faith and Mr. Bertram had worked several hours arranging and rearranging funds to find the best way for Mr. Bertram's money to be spent. The papers which now lay on Mr. Clarke's desk were the results of those hours. They had been mostly good hours. Faith had to admit she had enjoyed her time discussing money and various other topics with Mr. Bertram, although there had been one point of unease.

"The business idea seems sound?" Faith leaned forward and propped her elbows on Mr. Clarke's desk so she could get a better look at the numbers, just to make sure she was not remembering them incorrectly. "I think things are arranged so that no ill will befall Mr. Bertram's present estate holdings." Even if it was a risk which she did not feel comfortable with recommending.

"Yes, yes. Everything is very well accounted for." Mr. Clarke wore a pleased expression.

"It is not too great a risk?" Faith asked.

"No more than any other investment. There will be a healthy return on his investment as soon as the business begins to turn a profit."

"Durward is exceptionally good at what he does," Tom inserted.

"Oh, indeed!" Mr. Clarke agreed. "I would not hesitate to send investors in his direction."

Faith blew out a breath. "But a merchant is often..." She shook her head. "Gentlemen do not always see to it that their accounts are reconciled."

"Aye, it is a risk, Miss Eldridge," Mr. Clarke agreed.

"But no greater than any other," Robert said. "I would offer up my own funds to this venture if I were allowed."

Her brother was standing beside Mr. Clarke's desk and catching her eye, lifted an accusatory brow. They had discussed, or rather argued, over that very thing last night after Mr. Bertram had left. Robert just could not make the connection between Mrs. Johns' current state of living and the accounts Mr. Johns had left unpaid upon his demise. To Robert, it was simply a matter of an unfeeling relation and heir which had caused Mrs. Johns' decline into lowered circumstances. But, in Faith's opinion, had Mr. Johns set up his accounts better when he was alive, there could have been more left for those he loved. She was certain of it, and his love of new coats and hats, as well as furnishings and such, were, in her mind, the cause.

She glanced over her shoulder at Mr. Bertram. His handsome features were drawn with concern, and his eyes seemed to be questioning her.

"Very well," she said as she straightened. "I am certain this venture will be profitable if you three gentlemen say it is." She tried to keep the sharpness she felt out of her tone but did not succeed.

"That is not what we are saying," Robert grumbled.

"Are you not? Is this then, a bad investment?"

Her brother growled. "You know of what I speak. You are not a foolish chit."

"And yet you toss my concerns aside as if I were." She pressed her lips together and pulled them into a tight smile. "Forgive me. I seem to be not quite myself today."

Why it concerned her so much that someone so utterly unrelated to her as Mr. Bertram might lose some pounds on an investment should things go badly was beyond her. She should be dispassionately removed from the whole affair. They should only be numbers on a page, but they were not. She cared whether Mr. Bertram succeeded or not simply because he had become a friend.

"Oh, no. You are very much yourself," Robert muttered.

It took a great deal of fortitude for Faith to not reply as she wished. "Thank you, Mr. Clarke. Your service is always appreciated."

She rose to leave. They were done. The decisions were made. All that remained to be done was to wait until either the profits or losses began to come in. She prayed that the losses would be small if there were to be losses at all. Mr. Bertram had trusted her. Her brow furrowed. That was it. Mr. Bertram's success was her success for she had been the advisor behind the decisions – save for that last one, of course.

"I would like you to meet Mr. Durward." Tom smiled up at her from where he still sat in front of Mr. Clarke's desk. "I think it would help put your mind at ease."

"I do not distrust your friend," Faith said quietly. "I distrust the gentlemen who will shop at his establishment."

Tom rose and stood before her, close enough that she had to look up at him. Close enough that she could feel that familiar tingling warmth that seemed to want to draw her closer to him.

"I assure you that you need only trust Gabe."

His soft tone and expression nearly elicited a sigh from her. It was no wonder Mr. Bertram had the reputation he had of being a charmer. He was speaking of business deals and partners and yet, she wished to sigh like some besotted young miss – at his words.

"He will not allow anyone to take advantage of him or his friends. I would bet my life on it." There was confidence in his tone.

"Do you gamble often, Mr. Bertram?" It was not what she wanted to say. However, she could not say she would go anywhere he offered if he would only keep smiling so that dimple showed. That certainly would not do.

"Perhaps a bit more than you."

Faith blinked. "I do not gamble, Mr. Bertram."

"Each of your investments is a risk – that is a gamble. Not one of them is a sure thing."

"They are necessary," Faith replied quickly.

"I do not disagree," Tom assured her. "And you take a risk with your reputation and future by dressing as you do to come to this establishment, and though I do not know why you were dressed as you were yesterday when I saw you, I am going to venture a guess that your costume was due to taking some risk."

"That is also necessary." Faith bit down on the full retort she wished to make. If it were not for gentlemen who spent to excess or toss their inheritance away on some foolish pleasure, she would not have to take either of the risks he mentioned.

"Necessary gambles."

"I do not gamble. I invest, and I see to those for whom I care."

Tom shook his head. "What you do, you do for noble reasons. However, you are still taking a chance and putting yourself at risk." He grasped her by her shoulders and held her gaze steady. "Not all gambles are unworthy of the risk. Mr. Durward is worth the risk to my finances. The investment will not harm my estate further than making it take longer for me to recoup what I have lost."

If he were Robert, she would point out to him that his ability to choose risks wisely was what led to his loss. However, he was not Robert, and she did not wish to disparage his friend by saying his friend was a poor risk. She did not even know this friend beyond what she had heard from Mr. Bertram. Perhaps he was correct. Perhaps she did need to meet this Mr. Durward.

"You are right."

"Oh, ho! Well done, Bertram!" Robert cried. "Those are not frequently used words in my sister's vocabulary."

Faith glared at her brother and mouthed the words shut up at him.

"I can understand why with you as her brother."

Mr. Bertram smiled down at her and slowly removed his hands from her shoulders, almost as if he did not wish to remove them, which suit her quite well. She was not in any hurry to have him unhand her.

"A fine thing that is!" Robert protested. "I defended your decision to her, you know, and this is the thanks I get for my efforts?"

Mr. Bertram shook his head and rolled his eyes. "If you would be quiet for a moment, Eldridge, your sister might be able to tell me about what I am correct."

There was a bit of huffing from her brother, but he held his tongue.

"I think I must meet Mr. Durward to feel at ease. I have little to go on for my part. The word of a friend, such as yourself, may be true in fact or it may be true due to the admiration a friend holds for another friend."

"Then, it is me you do not trust."

Faith's eyes grew wide. "No, that is not what I meant. I only meant that a friend will often see the best in another friend and may be blind to any deficit." She sighed. "I am not making it any better, am I?"

Mr. Bertram chuckled and shook his head. "I do understand your concern, though I would wish for my word to be taken as surety."

"I am sorry," Faith muttered. "I truly did not mean to disparage either you or your friend."

She would be quite happy to sink through the floor and escape through some door on the lower floor even if it meant the possibility of running into cobwebs or seeing a rat. That would be better than remaining here and wishing to cry over her words. Cry! Of all the foolish things to wish to do! As if a few salty drops of water could atone for her dreadful words.

"Truly, Miss Eldridge. I do not find fault in your caution." Mr. Bertram's words were gentle, as was the look in his eye.

"I do," Robert muttered.

"Shut up, Eldridge."

Faith could not stop the grin that Mr. Bertram's words

brought to her lips. She had so wished to say that very thing to her brother. "When might we be able to call on your friend?"

"I am expected for tea."

"Today?"

Mr. Bertram nodded. "I shall not give him a farthing until you have seen for yourself that I am not making an unwise investment." His lips, which Faith had to admit seemed to draw her attention often, quirked upward. "However, you may wish to go home and change first."

Robert laughed as Faith's cheeks burned.

"Yes... of course..." she stammered, "but I have not been invited by Mr. Durward."

"He will not be offended. However, I must warn you about his mother." Mr. Bertram gathered his papers from the desk. "She is a bit of a mother hen, and anyone who enters her door runs the risk of becoming one of her chicks." He paused at the door before opening it. "Are you willing to take the gamble?"

"It seems it is necessary," Faith replied with a saucy grin, "but I do not gamble, Mr. Bertram." Nor did she flirt, and yet she seemed to be doing a fine job of that.

His eyes scanned her from head to toe and back again, causing her insides to threaten to burst into flame. How did he do that with merely a look?

"No, of course not, Miss Eldridge," he said. "Of course not."

Chapter 9

"He will not be offended," Tom whispered to Miss Eldridge as she shifted from foot to foot while they waited for the Durward's door to open.

He wished to remove her hand from his arm so that he could place that arm around her shoulders and draw her closer to his side. But that would not do.

Her brother had permitted her to attend him with only a maid as their chaperone. Should that chaperone return home with a poor report, any hope of spending another pleasurable few hours seated beside Robert's sister with an account book in front of them would be lost. And Tom desperately needed her help with his finances almost as much as he was beginning to crave her presence.

That last fact was somewhat disturbing. For one thing, he was not yet ready to begin a search for a wife in earnest. Added to that, his attraction to her seemed opposed to his desire to leave his former self behind, for he thought entirely too often about how her lips must taste and how the softness of her form pressed against him would feel.

"Oh, Mr. Bertram!" Mrs. Durward's greeting interrupted Tom's thoughts before they could travel any further down an inappropriate road. "You have brought a friend!" Mrs. Durward stood behind the butler, peering out at the two people in front of her door.

"This is Miss Eldridge."

Despite his best efforts, when Miss Eldridge removed her hand from Tom's arm to enter the house, Tom instinctively placed his hand on the small of her back to guide her. However, no sooner had his hand connected with her person than he snatched it away.

"Miss Eldridge, this is Mrs. Durward."

Faith's eyes looked first at him, her gaze dropping to his hand, and then with a smile, she turned her eyes toward Mrs. Durward.

He would apologize later. Clasping his hands behind his back, Tom followed Faith into the house as she gave her greeting to Mrs. Durward.

"Mr. Bertram did not think it too forward of me to accompany him. He is very desirous that I meet his friend, Mr. Durward."

"I assure you it is not forward at all," Mrs. Durward said, barely refraining, Tom noticed, from helping Miss Eldridge remove her coat.

Tom placed his hat on the table near the door as he always did when he entered and handed his coat to the butler, who had also gathered Miss Eldridge's things.

"Miss Eldridge has been helping me with my finances."

Mrs. Durward's eyes lit with curiosity. "You like numbers?"

"I do."

"My son always loved numbers," Mrs. Durward said. "He would count everything when he was just a boy. He would even place his biscuits in groups and count by groups. And now he does very well in business. It is as if he was designed for it from birth."

"I was not so blessed," Tom said.

Gabe's mother smiled at him. "You have other talents." She did not elaborate on that fact but rather turned back to Faith. "Gabriel also loved to set things sailing." She sighed. "And now he owns ships, and soon he will have his own warehouse and a store."

"You must be very proud of him."

Miss Eldridge gave Tom an amused smile as they followed Mrs. Durward into the sitting room.

"Oh, I am. I always have been," she replied. Then, she turned and took Faith's hands. "You are not so very cold, but I would suggest a seat nearer the fire just to be safe."

Faith's eyes had grown wide at the gesture. "Of course."

"Mr. Bertram prefers this settee." Mrs. Durward lowered her voice. "There is a footstool near, in case he needs it."

"I see." Faith pressed her lips together, but Tom could see amusement dancing in her eyes.

"A mother hen," he whispered.

"Indeed," Faith whispered in reply.

"There is room for two on the settee, and it is not too far from the fire," Tom suggested. He would be much more comfortable with Miss Eldridge near him rather than the fire.

"I am not cold."

"That matters not in this room. You will see. Mrs. Durward is used to the heat of India."

"Is that where she gets her dark looks?" Faith whispered.

Tom nodded. "You do not object to her, do you?"

Faith shook her head. "No, though I am certain some might think I should." Her eyes grew wide as Gabe entered the room. "Oh, my! I knew you had said he was injured, but I had not thought..." She fell silent as Gabe approached, hobbling across the room on his crutch and with one arm visibly bandaged.

"I never did tell you how Durward sustained his injuries, did I?" Tom said.

She shook her head.

"Someone attempted to steal my boat with the lady I loved on board." Gabe had reached them in time to hear Tom's question. "My injuries are not so bad as his since mine will heal, and his will not." Gabe bowed as best he could to Miss Eldridge and then looked at Tom inquisitively.

Slowly he turned his eyes away from Faith, whose

mouth had dropped open for a moment. No doubt she was shocked by Gabe's blunt explanation of his injuries.

"Durward, this is Miss Eldridge. Miss Eldridge, this is my good friend, Mr. Gabriel Durward."

"It is a pleasure to meet you, Mr. Durward."

"Likewise," Gabe said before taking a seat near the settee. "Miss Crawford was going to join us today, but she was uncertain how long she and her sister would be delivering their goods to the foundling's hospital." He turned to Faith. "They sew clothing and blankets for the children."

"That is lovely."

The truth of her words shone in the delight that suffused her features. Once again, Tom was reminded of an angel by how her beauty radiated from something intangible within her.

"Miss Eldridge is the lady who is helping me with my finances," Tom explained to Gabe while not removing his eyes from Faith. "I thought it would be good for you to meet."

"So, you are the expert that Mr. Clarke selected to help Bertram?"

"I am." A faint pink stained her lovely cheeks.

"We were just at Mr. Clarke's earlier today. My books appear to be in order for the time being, and Mr. Clarke was pleased with them. However, Miss Eldridge holds some trepidation about the risk involved in investing in a store." He smiled reassuringly when Faith turned concerned eyes toward him.

"I am glad to hear it," Gabe said, settling back into his chair with only a small grimace.

"You are?"

Gabe nodded in reply to Faith's startled question.

"There are risks to such a thing."

Her eyes narrowed. "Are you attempting to placate me?"

Tom chuckled. "Durward rarely placates anyone when it comes to business ventures."

"Even a lady?"

"Even a lady," Gabe replied as Tom could not, for he had gotten somewhat lost in the fluttering of lashes over blue eyes.

"I like that you are direct, Miss Eldridge. It makes me feel better about having sent Bertram in your direction."

Mrs. Durward, accompanied by the tea things, entered the room, and talk of business arrangements died for some time while cups of tea were distributed, and everyone had assured her that they did not require anything further. Then, the conversation shifted to more mundane things for a time.

Tom watched Faith as she spoke to Mrs. Durward about the dampness of the weather and how it made the cold so much more unbearable.

Miss Eldridge was at ease here with his friends. She glanced his direction a few times, but for the most part, her attention was fully on Mrs. Durward, and her comments did not sound empty. There was a compassion within Miss Eldridge that was incapable of being contained. Her brow furrowed with concern as Mrs. Durward spoke of her son's injuries, while Tom chuckled at Gabe's grumble over it.

"Injuries should not be taken lightly," Faith said to Gabe. "Your mother is quite correct. An injury that is not tended to as it ought to be can lead to some dire consequences. You have only to look to your friend to learn such a thing."

"Bertram?" Gabe asked.

Faith nodded. "If Mr. Bertram's injury had been tended to properly when it was first sustained rather than days afterward, he might not have developed the fever he did." She turned to Mrs. Durward. "It nearly claimed his life."

Mrs. Durward gasped. Tom had never told Gabe's mother precisely how serious the injury resulting in his need for a cane had been.

"A fall where one sustains breaks and bruises is one thing, to acquire an unsightly gash in the process opens the body up to a myriad of ravages. That is what caused Mr. Bertram's illness, I am nearly certain of it, as was the surgeon."

Tom lowered his cup slowly to the table. Miss Eldridge seemed to know a great deal about his accident and injury.

"He was fortunate to survive," Faith added.

"Thanks to an angel," Tom muttered.

"An angel, you say?" Durward asked.

"As you know," Tom answered.

"*I* do not know," Mrs. Durward said.

Tom tipped his head and closed his eyes so that he could only faintly see Miss Eldridge through his lashes. She did look similar to the maid who had sat next to his bed.

His eyes flew open.

Maid!

A maid had sat next to his bed while he was ill. That was why seeing Miss Eldridge dressed like a maid yesterday had seemed as if it had happened before and why his mind would not allow him to stop wondering about her purpose in dressing in such a fashion.

"What were you doing yesterday?" he asked.

Faith blinked. "I did many things yesterday." Her gaze lowered to watch her fingers break a biscuit into tiny pieces on her plate.

"When I saw you."

"I was at home, reading."

She was avoiding. He was right. She was the maid who had cared for him. He shook his head. He was not going to accept such an easy deflection. "Not then, before. When I was out riding."

"I was visiting a friend."

"You were dressed as a maid."

Her eyes shifted from him to look at their companions. "It is easier to travel to certain areas of town when one looks as if she has little money, and at times, I will go to a store to purchase things for my friends, and..." She pressed her lips together as if she did not wish to continue. "It is easier to do that if the shopkeepers think you are a servant," she finished.

"And it is necessary for you to do that?" She had said it was necessary for her to be dressed as she was when they had spoken of it in Mr. Clarke's office.

She nodded, but she did not look at him.

"Why is it necessary?" Tom pressed.

"I would rather not say." She lifted defiant eyes to him.

"Your friend is not well, is she?"

Pain filled her eyes as she shook her head. "Her body is mending."

He would love to know what had happened to this friend, but he would not press her further. Indeed, he had, from the looks he saw on Gabe's and Mrs. Durward's faces, likely pressed beyond where he should have as it was. "She sang beautifully."

Faith shook her head. "That was her student, and it is Olivia's mother who is not well." Once again, she pressed her lips together to keep from speaking.

"She is fortunate to have you." Tom kept his tone gentle and smiled softly at his angel. "When I was ill, there was a maid who sat by my side, keeping watch over me, seeing that I had all I needed in order to have the best chance at recovery. Therefore, I know just how fortunate your friend is to have you seeing to her care."

Her eyes searched his, questioning him. He flicked a brow while tilting his head and shrugging in response. Her throat rose and fell as she swallowed, her eyes growing just the tiniest bit wide and her breath quickening. She understood that he knew the maid had been her.

"I was not fully aware of my surrounding for several days," Tom said to Mrs. Durward. "But I remember there was an angel who sat by me and sang to me. I cannot tell you how comforting it was." Just as it was comforting now to remember how someone had cared for him when he had done nothing to deserve such care. His behavior at the time had been justly rewarded with his injury and subsequent illness. But his angel – Miss Eldridge — had provided mercy for his wayward soul.

"I am glad you had someone to tend to you," said Mrs. Durward.

"As am I," Gabe added.

"And you do not know who it was?" Mrs. Durward was excessively curious – much like her son, although a quick glance at that son let Tom know that Gabe seemed aware of the unspoken discussion that had occurred.

Tom held Miss Eldridge's gaze as he answered Mrs. Durward's question.

"No," he lied. "My friend was not certain who it was either."

That was also a lie, though until this afternoon, Tom had not known it was not the truth. Of course, Robert would conceal such a thing. Young ladies did not spend days sitting in a gentleman's bedroom without running the risk of having her reputation thoroughly and utterly ruined.

And Miss Eldridge claimed to not like high risk investments or gambling!

He shook his head and returned to his tea thankful that she had wagered her reputation to save his life.

Chapter 10

"Do you feel more at ease, having met Mr. Durward?" Tom asked as he handed Faith into the carriage an agonizing half hour later.

How she had managed to not wither away from the mortification of his realizing she had been his nurse when ill must have been an act of Providence. Whether it was a miraculous act or an act of extreme cruelty designed to punish her for her actions, she was uncertain. She knew she pushed the bounds of propriety at times, but she had always done so with what she considered noble reasons.

"He would not lead you astray," she managed to say in a tone of voice that did not give any hint at the quivering she felt within.

"Then you approve of the venture?"

She nodded. "It is your money."

"That is not what I asked." Tom stopped half in and half out of the vehicle. "I will not invest a farthing without your approval." He continued entering the carriage.

"Why?" Tears threatened, and she blinked rapidly against them. "Why does my approval mean so much?"

Her emotions were little more than frayed bits of rope at present. She should smile, nod, and grant him her blessing whether she understood why he sought it or not. She should remain calm and rational, but all of those things which she should do were not within her power to do.

She turned to her maid. "Would you please ask to ride with the driver? You can wear my coat if yours is not warm enough, but I must speak with Mr. Bertram about his investments."

"Of course, miss."

Faith held a hand up to forestall anything that Mr. Bertram might say while they waited for the maid to exit the carriage.

"Do you need my pelisse?" Faith asked before the door closed.

"There is a blanket, miss," the footman at the door replied. "I will see that she has that."

"Thank you." Faith did not shift her eyes from the door for half a minute after it closed. Then, straightening her spine, she prepared herself to have what would likely be a frank and very discomfiting discussion with Mr. Bertram.

"May I speak now?" He was looking at her curiously. He no doubt was questioning her sanity.

Faith nodded.

"I do not know why your approval means so much, but it does."

"That is not an answer." She could feel her emotions welling up in an unmanageable mound.

"It most certainly is," Tom assured her.

"But it does not help me at all. What if I am wrong? What if everything I have suggested to you causes you to lose your funds? I am not infallible." She rubbed her hands back and forth on her knees until he stopped her from doing so by covering her hands with his.

"No, you are not infallible, but you are compassionate. A compassionate person would not lead me astray. Durward would not, and neither would you."

"But what if I do?"

"Do you mean to?"

Faith shook her head.

"Am I not capable of making my own choices?"

"Of course, you are, but I do not understand how that follows."

"Just as I choose to accept Durward's advice based on my belief that he would not knowingly cause me harm, so, too, I choose to accept your advice. If I lose money, it is because of *my* choice." His eyes did not waver from hers. "Do you approve of the venture?"

She nodded. "Mr. Durward is..." She shrugged. "Everything you have said he is."

The smile that slipped slowly from his lips to his eyes eased her worries somewhat.

"I..." She lowered her eyes to their joined hands. This part of their discussion was going to be even more difficult to have while keeping her emotions contained. "I..." She paused to breathe. "I... I wanted to thank you for not telling the others that it was me who sat with you at my brother's estate."

He removed one of his hands from hers and cupped her cheek, brushing the corner of her eye with the pad of his thumb. "Why did you sit with me?"

She shrugged. "How could I not? I arrived to find my brother gone and a gravely ill stranger in his place. There were so few staff. I could not tax them any more than they already were." She shrugged again. "And I could not allow you to die."

A tear escaped despite her desperate blinking, and she closed her eyes in an attempt to contain the others. She could not have done anything differently than she had done, except, perhaps, hire some additional hands for a few days, but then, she had not had the funds with her nor the authority to spend such sums.

Soft lips pressed against her forehead. She should be startled by the gesture, but she was not. She welcomed its sweetness.

"I have long wished to meet you and tell you how very thankful I am for what you did for me," Tom whispered.

"You mustn't tell anyone else this, but it was your care that made me long to better myself as I remembered you while convalescing at Mansfield. My father thinks I have just finally come to my senses of my own accord – assisted by the gravity of my illness."

Faith dared to peek up at him. She could not name the emotion she saw in his eyes, but it captivated her, and she could not look away.

"But it was not the nearly dying part which caused my change – though I have claimed it is to many people and will likely continue to do so. It was the wishing to live and to once again find the comfort I felt when you sat beside me. That is what has wrought a change in my heart." His thumb caressed her lips, his eyes following it. He leaned toward her. "If my finances were what they should be..." His thumb passed over her lips again. "I could find that comfort once again." His head inched closer to hers, his eyes on her lips.

He was going to kiss her. Her heart and breath quickened. She knew she would not stop him.

Then, just before his lips should have touched hers, he pulled back, removed his hand from her cheek and apologized.

Apologized!

As if she were not welcoming of his actions.

She thought to tell him she did not find his actions in the least bit offensive, but she did not. She simply muttered an acceptance of his regret and attempted not to feel the sting of it all while brushing at the tears which would not keep from falling.

He pressed his handkerchief into the hand which rested on her lap. "Forgive me. I did not mean to overwhelm you." He shrugged and looked excessively distressed.

"I am merely overwrought by all that has happened," she fibbed. It seemed a far better thing to say than *How dare you make me think you might care for me and then dash my hopes? Do you not know that I, too, have thought of you almost daily since the day I discovered you at my brother's estate?*

No, she could not say that. It smacked too much of desperation, and a lady must retain some trace of dignity.

"Did my brother, Edmund, meet you?"

Faith remembered the day Mr. Edmund Bertram had arrived. He was quite beside himself with concern, and Faith had been happy to know that Mr. Bertram had family who cared for him as much as Robert cared for her.

"I did, but not as me. I was just a maid – Eliza. My name is Faith Elizabeth, so it was not a complete untruth."

Mr. Bertram shook his head and chuckled. "For a lady who claims not to like risk, you seem to take it on quite easily."

"Easily? I should think not! I feared discovery every day. What if one of the servants did not remember the role I was playing and said something to reveal the truth? What if they carried tales to other servants who shared them with their masters and mistresses?" She blew out a breath. "There is one less worry now, I suppose."

"What is that?"

"Each time we meet, I no longer need to fret over whether you will discover it was me who took care of you. Of course, there is less need for us to meet," she added quickly.

He had just apologized for nearly kissing her. He might not wish to call on her when there were no account books which needed her attention. They would still need to meet occasionally to review how his investments were doing. One could not just place their money with a stockbroker and forget to watch it. That was a sure way to lose money.

His brow furrowed. "If that is what you wish."

"No, no, I am not saying I do not wish for us to meet. I am only saying that the hardest part of sorting out a plan for your money is over. We need only monitor now and review on occasion and so on. I am certain you have many other things which will need your attention what with the store and warehouse and all."

"But you would welcome me if I called?"

"Most happily, yes. However. I thought you might not wish to call, and I did not want you to feel obligated." She pressed her lips together. She was babbling nervously. "I am most curious to hear how your venture progresses with Mr. Durward," she added after a moment's pause to calm her thoughts enough to produce rational speech rather than rambling and rapid sentences that strung themselves together like some child's haphazardly created crown of daisies.

The carriage slowed to a stop.

She was home and nearly in one piece.

No that was not true. She was not close to being in one piece; it was just that all her broken, confused bits were still inside one body.

She allowed Mr. Bertram to help her from the carriage and see her to her door. Then, with a sigh, she unpinned her hat and removed her gloves and pelisse, leaving them with her maid as she made her way to Robert's study.

"Did Mr. Durward meet with your approval?" Robert said, looking up from the book he was reading near the hearth.

Faith nodded as she sat down in the chair across from him.

Her brother snapped his book closed and sat up straighter. "What happened?"

"What do you mean?" She knew what he meant.

"You are quiet, and if I am not mistaken, it looks as if you have been crying." He pointed to his eye. "Your eyes are not as clear as they should be."

Faith blew out a breath and flopped backward in her chair. "He knows it was me."

"Bertram knows you were the one who cared for him?"

Faith nodded. "He was grateful, of course." Grateful enough to almost kiss her until he thought better of it.

"Does he know that you saw him undressed?"

Faith shook her head. "Although I would venture, he will eventually figure that out as well. I mentioned his gash." She shook her head again, this time in reproach of her careless mistake.

Robert groaned.

"I know," Faith commiserated with her brother.

The gash was located above Mr. Bertram's knee. There was no way for her to have seen it unless he was not wearing breeches. And sooner or later he would deduce that the poultices which had warmed his chest were likely placed there by her as well.

"He will not tell anyone." She was certain of that since he did not divulge her secret to Mr. Durward and his mother.

"Well," said Robert, "I should hope not, but if he does, then I shall have to insist he saves your reputation just as you saved his life."

"I will not be forced on any man, Robert."

"You may have no choice, and there are far less agreeable men upon whom you could be foisted, you know."

Despite the heaviness which lay on her heart, Faith chuckled softly at the way her brother folded his hands across his middle and looked every inch like her father when he was preparing to lecture one of his offspring. Most often it had been Robert.

"I know," she said.

The room fell silent until, finally, Faith admitted what was pressing so heavily on her. "I am not opposed to being tied to Mr. Bertram." She cared for him and not just as a friend. She had not known it until he had almost kissed her, and from the way her heart hurt, there was no denying it now.

Her brother's eyebrows sprang toward his hairline.

"I am opposed to him being tied to me." She bit her quivering lower lip and shrugged. "I think I shall take a rest before dinner." She rose and crossed to the door. "Actually, I think I shall have a bath and then eat my dinner in my room before going to bed early."

"Faith," her brother called to her.

She turned and smiled quickly at him. "I know. You think any gentleman would be fortunate to have me, but you are my brother. Your judgment is skewed."

"It is not skewed. You are annoying, but you are also quite wonderful," he called after her, causing her to smile once again.

If only Mr. Bertram thought she was as wonderful as her brother did. She would know soon, she supposed. If he did indeed call on her as he claimed he wished to do, then and only then, would she allow herself to hope.

Chapter 11

"Gentlemen, might I present you with a lease for your approval." Mr. Gardiner placed a document on the desk in his office.

It had been two days since Tom had last seen Gabe. The man should be at home, but he was not. He was here, leading Waller and Tom through a business deal.

"The building is only a street away from here. It is not as large as this one, but it can store a great quantity of goods. I know because I was the sole occupant of that very building before acquiring this one. I have only just purchased it from the former owner and can assure you that your landlord will be a good one." Mr. Gardiner chuckled. "He might be a trifle demanding, however."

Gabe had taken up the document and was reading through it. His and Waller's investments in this venture were the most critical. They were playing with money that, should it be lost, the impact would be felt more greatly than it would for Tom. Tom's estate was secure. It was not as strong as it would be once this investment started producing returns, but it was not in danger of failing if the investment were to sustain a loss. Miss Eldridge had seen to that.

However, if one were to examine this trio of men seated before Gardiner's desk more carefully, Tom and Waller were actually, at present, the gentlemen with the most to lose. Waller had to prove himself financially before the father of the lady he loved would allow him to court her. Tom's predicament was similar, although there was no father to please in his case. Tom needed to prove to himself that he was worthy of his angel, now that he had found her. Therefore, it was with great interest that Tom waited to hear what Gabe thought of the building on offer.

"I will not allow you to sign it now," Gardiner said when Gabe was about halfway through the agreement. "I would not want you to sign it without consulting a solicitor. I had mine draw that up, but it would be less than wise for you to accept my word that it is a good agreement. There could have been an error – some item which might have been neglected, though I cannot think of any. I assure you that I take my reputation as a fair and honest businessman very seriously."

Gabe smiled. "That is what I like about you, Gardiner. You have always dealt honestly with me. Never a late payment. Never a suggestion of a hidden deal. Would that all businessmen were as you are." He returned to reading and the room fell silent again until he had finished. "It looks to be sound, but I agree. It is never a poor idea to take a precaution on something such as this. I wish to keep you as a friend as well as a business associate, and that can only be done if we both do our own thinking and assuring."

"Trust with verification." Gardiner's smile was as wide as Gabe's.

The fact that these two men seemed to be cut from a bolt of the same cloth was reassuring to Tom. He needed his money to be handled carefully. His future happiness hung in the balance. And if he were being completely honest, he hoped that that future was not too far off. If he could see a steady return, he could, with Miss Eldridge's assistance, calculate when he might be free of his debt and ready to leave every remaining facet of his past behind him as he moved forward unfettered.

"I will have my solicitor look at this as soon as possible, and if all is as it appears, it will be returned to you signed with all haste." Gabe offered the document to Waller. "I do not speak out of turn, do I?" He asked his companions.

Tom shook his head. "I trust you."

"As do I," Waller agreed, looking up briefly from the papers he held.

"You will, of course, read this?" Gabe nodded toward the papers Waller held.

Tom chuckled. "I would not wish to inform Miss Eldridge I had handed over my money without carefully scrutinizing the details."

"Miss Eldridge?" There was a curious twinkle in Gardiner's eye.

"She has been assisting me with my books." Tom's ear burned slightly with the admission, but not because he was seeking help from a female. No, it was his need to seek any help at all in matters he should understand which caused his discomfort.

"A lady with a keen mind! There is nothing better," Gardiner said. "My wife is such a woman, as are a few of my nieces." He scratched his cheek as he contemplated something. "Do you know Mr. Darcy?"

Tom shook his head and shrugged. "I have heard of him, but I do not know him."

"This Miss Eldridge is a gentleman's daughter?"

"She is, although she has been left to her brother's care."

Gardiner nodded. "Sadly, that is not as unusual as it should be, but I only asked to make certain this young woman was of the same circles as my niece, Elizabeth." Gardiner's expression grew serious. "She is settling into her role as Mrs. Darcy very well. There is no reason for me to ask this but for selfish reasons. She has always lacked friends who were as bright as she was, and I thought if, sometime, this Miss Eldridge could meet my niece, it might be good for Lizzy. Of course, I do not know what Miss Eldridge is like, so I cannot say for certain they would get along well just because they both possess keen minds."[1]

"It would be something to consider," Tom agreed as he

accepted the lease agreement from Gabe and began to look it over while Mr. Gardiner spoke to Waller and Durward about the building and his nieces.

"This also looks thorough to me," Tom said when he had completed his perusal of the document.

"Then it is just a matter of having my solicitor look over the documentation and for us to look over the building. I had hoped to find a warehouse first and then a store, but if you say this place has a good bit of storage, then perhaps the warehouse could wait a few months. I can tolerate my current situation for a time." Gabe pushed to his feet with the help of his crutch.

"My carriage is out front, Mr. Gardiner," Tom offered.

~*~*~

"It is a very good-looking building," Tom said later as he sat in the Eldridge's drawing room. "Waller is considering taking up residence in the home above the store. It would not cost him more than he pays now where he is, and it would give us someone to watch over the establishment."

"And it all rests on Mr. Durward's solicitor's approval of the agreement?" Robert asked.

Tom nodded. "I could be earning back my losses in a very short time." That was the most thrilling bit. "I will not have much to do with the running of the business,

1. The Gardiners and Darcys in this book are the Gardiners and Darcys from Two Days Before Christmas, A Pride and Prejudice Variation by Leenie Brown

of course. I shall leave that to the tradesmen with experience."

"You seem eager to begin," Robert said with a laugh.

"I am," Tom admitted. He sucked in a breath and blew it out slowly. "I am eager for a very specific reason."

"What is that?"

"I cannot begin to consider taking a wife until I have repaid my debts or am well on my way to repaying them. I wish to leave my entire past behind me, you see, and those debts are the final reminders of who I once was."

"Other than the leg," Robert inserted.

Tom nodded. Even if his leg did heal to the point of never causing him pain again, he would always have the scar on his thigh. His brow furrowed. "Did you tell your sister about the gash on my leg?"

Robert shifted uneasily. "No, I was at a cockfight. The... um... surgeon must have spoken to her about it."

Tom tipped his head and studied his friend. "You do not know?"

Robert clamped his mouth shut and shook his head.

"Then, I shall have to ask her. Did you say she would be home soon?"

That made Robert squirm even more. There was something Tom's friend was not telling him.

"I could not say how soon she will return. I only know it will be before dinner."

"She saw it?" That was the only explanation which would cause Robert to squirm as he did.

"Saw what?"

Robert was not meeting his eyes. Tom suspected he had hit upon the true way in which Miss Eldridge knew of his injury.

"The gash on my leg."

"She may have."

"May have or did?" Tom pressed.

"I cannot say."

From the look on his friend's face, Robert was telling the truth. However, Tom was certain Robert's inability to clarify had little to do with whether or not he knew the answer and a great deal to do with not wishing to divulge any further information about his sister.

"You must not ask her," Robert begged, putting to rest all of Tom's questions. "Please."

"Very well, I will not ask her – for now," he added just to taunt his friend as he wondered just how much of his person had been exposed to Miss Eldridge while he was ill. A smile curled his lips. There was one person from whom he could likely gain his answers. His man had been with him. Surely, his valet would know more information about his time at Robert's estate than his friend would since Robert had not been there. "I am grateful for her assistance no matter how unclothed I might have been when she rendered it."

"And I must apologize once again for leaving you."

"I believe that is the first time you have apologized," Tom said. "Other than in that letter you wrote to me when I was at Mansfield."

Robert shook his head. "Perhaps it is the first time I have spoken the words to you, but I promise you that I have been reprimanded and required to repent of my actions many, many times. My sister thought it reprehensible – as it was – and will not allow me to forget my lapse in good sense."

"She is very caring."

"That she is. Take today, for instance. Do you know where she is?"

Tom shook his head.

"Shopping with a friend."

How was shopping a demonstration of a lady's caring nature?

"And do you know what she will buy for herself?" Robert continued.

"I am certain I do not know." If she were like most ladies, it would be dresses, bonnets, lace, gloves, and so forth. But Robert's sister was not like other ladies, and he knew that she had put limits on her purchasing to save money. She had told him about her retrenching.

"Nothing. Not one thing. But she will purchase needles and thread and likely some small gift for Mrs. Johns and Olivia."

Tom's brow furrowed. "Who are Mrs. Johns and Olivia?"

"Friends she has known since she was in leading strings." Robert stared off toward the window. "I should not allow it, and I would not if my sister were not as determined as she is, but she visits them often – on her own, although I am invited to visit as soon as Mrs. Johns is well enough."

This Mrs. Johns must be the friend Miss Eldridge was visiting the day he saw her dressed as a maid. He should not pry. She had been very clear about not wishing to tell him why she felt it necessary to visit them as she did. But there was one thing he just could not do without knowing.

"How did she become friends with someone who lives in that part of town? I mean it is not the poorest section, but it is not here."

"The Johns' were our neighbours before Mr. Johns had his accident. They have only been reduced to living as they are since. Mr. Johns' heir was only so generous since there were debts that needed settling. I do not wish to speak ill of the dead, mind you, but Mr. Johns did enjoy a new set of clothes."

And Olivia, Miss Johns, was reduced to taking in students. Things were beginning to make sense to Tom.

"Why will your sister buy needles and thread?" He was nearly certain he knew the answer.

"Mrs. Johns takes in sewing, and Faith helps her when she visits."

No wonder Miss Eldridge had been so concerned about his venture with Gabe. She witnessed the effects of over expenditure every time she visited her friend. If he had thought it was important to settle his debts before taking a wife before he had learned this information, he knew that it was doubly as important now, for he knew that the lady to whom he hoped to present his offer needed to see that he would not be like Mr. Johns.

Chapter 12

"My brother tells me you have settled on a building for part of your venture," Faith said as she took her place across from Mr. Bertram in the line of dancers.

She had not wanted to accept the invitation to this soiree tonight, but Robert had refused to attend without her. Her tears from yesterday evening seemed to have brought out all of his brotherly instincts – and despite his tendency to argue with her, as well as what she would call his lackadaisical approach to his future, he was not completely without some sort of proper sensibility.

She had been lectured in the carriage that she was to dance as often as asked. He would not be housing her forever, and she must begin searching in earnest for a husband. Then, clever boy that he was, he immediately sought out Mr. Bertram upon their arrival and announced he had a bit of a headache starting so he was not certain how long they would be staying.

If a girl was to be saddled with a numskull for a brother,

then Faith hoped that all such girls would be as fortunate as she and be graced with a loving dunderhead.

"We have."

The smile of achievement that spread across Mr. Bertram's face and lit his eyes caused her to sigh silently. She had done a good thing in giving him her blessing for this business undertaking for it appeared to have lifted the burden of his debts which he wore.

"I am glad to hear it," she replied.

He tipped his head slightly to one side, his brow furrowed.

"Truly," she assured him.

That returned his smile to his face just as the music began. For the duration of the set, they spoke in snatches about things of little significance – flowers, the weather, the crush of people, and so on. It was perhaps the longest and best conversation about the mundane things of the world in which Faith had ever taken part.

"I fear I will not be able to offer another set to you," Mr. Bertram said as they made their way from the floor. "Unless, of course, you do not mind strolling in the garden rather than dancing during the set."

He was limping more than usual. His leg must be hurting him most grievously. He had performed admirably while dancing, even if his hopping and skipping had been a trifle awkward at times when he began favouring one leg over the other.

"I am not a walking stick," Faith whispered, "but you may lean on me if you wish."

"I am certain I can make it to where I left my cane," he assured her with a smile.

"Do you even think it wise to walk in the garden? Would your leg not do better if you were to rest it?"

"You sounded very much like Mrs. Durward just now," he replied with a laugh.

"I promise not to instruct you to sit by the fire."

"Very well, then, shall we adjourn to the card room?"

She shook her head. "My brother has made me promise to dance as often as I am asked. I fear he might not think I was doing as he requested if I disappear from the ballroom. However, I would not be opposed to a short stroll of the garden and perhaps a small rest on a bench during some other dance tonight." It was almost as close as she dared come to declaring her feelings for him, there was one more thing she could say in that regard. "I was sorry to have missed your call yesterday."

They had reached the edge of the room, near the door to the corridor, and with a look over his shoulder, he led her into the hall.

"My brother..." she protested.

"Might be out here. I did not see him in the ballroom just now," Mr. Bertram replied with a grin.

"You know very well that he is not out here."

Mr. Bertram only shrugged in response, and Faith had

to admit that she was not at all displeased to be walking here with him instead of standing in the ballroom waiting for some gentleman to ask her to dance. There would be someone. There always was. She was no wallflower. Not even when she wished to be a wallflower rather than dancing with an unpleasant partner.

"Durward is arranging for a shipment of goods to be delivered to our store next week. Pardon me," Tom added as he stumbled and hopped once from bad leg to good leg after bumping against a gentleman.

The accident was her fault, and she should feel some remorse. However, she could not find it within herself to regret the way he had been looking at her rather than at where he was going.

"No harm has been done," the gentleman said.

"None at all," one of the ladies beside him agreed.

Faith expected to continue walking down the hall, but they did not.

"Are you Mr. Darcy?" Mr. Bertram asked.

"I am."

"Mr. Tom Bertram. And this is Miss Eldridge," Mr. Bertram said in introduction.

"It is a pleasure to meet you even if it was by accident," Mr. Darcy replied with a smile. "May I present my wife, Mrs. Darcy, and her sister, Miss Kitty Bennet, to you?"

The customary niceties of greeting were exchanged and

once again, Faith expected to continue walking but Mr. Bertram did not move.

"I have had the pleasure of meeting your uncle," Mr. Bertram said to Mrs. Darcy.

"Uncle Gardiner?" the lady asked in delighted surprise.

"Yes," Mr. Bertram replied. "I have entered into a bit of an investment with him."

Mrs. Darcy laughed. "That sounds like Uncle Gardiner. He is always conducting some sort of business."

"He is much like my friend," Mr. Bertram looked at Faith and added, "Mr. Durward."

"Then he must be lovely," Faith replied.

"My sister is in town visiting our aunt," Mrs. Darcy continued. "Perhaps we will cross paths again."

"I would welcome it," Tom replied.

"Do you do any charity work?" Mrs. Darcy asked eagerly.

Next to Faith, Mr. Bertram shook his head. "Currently, I do not, although my friend Mr. Edwards has attempted to bring me along when he goes to Mr. Gardiner's warehouse. However, Miss Eldridge does some private charity work, even though she would not call it such."

"You do?" Mrs. Darcy had not lost an ounce of animation, if possible, she might have gained some.

"I am not certain I do," Faith glanced at Mr. Bertram.

"Oh, she does," he said firmly. "However, she would call it doing what was necessary."

"That is such a good way to say it. Helping others, whether friend or stranger, is not a luxury."

Mr. Darcy cleared his throat, and Mrs. Darcy blushed, though her eyes seemed to sparkle even more than before.

"I have found charity work quite to my liking," she said apologetically, "and I find it hard to believe anyone else does not find it so." She opened her reticule and withdrew a card. "Miss Eldridge, this is likely too forward, but I would be pleased if you would call on me."

"She will question you about your charity work," Mr. Darcy cautioned Faith, who could not help noticing the pride in the man's eyes when he smiled at his wife.

Faith accepted the proffered card. "I would be happy to call, but there is not much to tell."

"Then we shall just have tea," Mrs. Darcy replied.

"It was good to meet you," Mr. Bertram said before he once again led Faith down the hall.

"Mr. Gardiner is the gentleman with the building?" Faith asked.

Mr. Bertram nodded.

"Mrs. Darcy seems nice."

"Her uncle thought you and she might find you have some similar interests."

Faith's brow furrowed. "You spoke of me to Mr. Gardiner?"

Again, Mr. Bertram nodded. "He knows you have helped me with my finances, and it seems Mrs. Darcy is also an intelligent lady. So, he thought perhaps you might suit each other."

"Is that why you introduced me to them?" She wasn't certain if she was pleased by this or not.

"Yes. Was that wrong of me to do?"

She shook her head. "I am uncertain."

"I apologize if I overstepped in my desire to see you..." He pressed his lips together.

"To see me what?" He could not just leave a sentence only partially spoken. She was not about to allow it.

"I have not seen you with or heard you speak of many friends. I thought perhaps with how silly I have found most of the ladies with whom I have spent a dance or an afternoon in a drawing room, and knowing how you are not at all like them, you might ... I have gone too far."

"You want to help me make friends?"

He grimaced.

"You thought about me that much?" She must have been in his thoughts a great deal if he was noticing things such as her lack of friends. "Thank you."

"Then I have not gone too far?"

"A trifle," Faith replied with a grin. "I do have friends. Not that any of them are in that ballroom. But I appreciate your concern for me."

"I would like to meet your friends," he replied. "It seems only right since you have already met Mr. Durward and you are related to Robert, which means you know, at least, two of my friends."

She loved how that dimple showed when he smiled.

"However, I will wait until your friend's mother has improved."

They walked three more paces to the end of the corridor where he turned to look at her before they retraced their steps toward the ballroom. Again, he was looking at her with that curious, mesmerizing expression he had worn in the carriage. And now, just as then, she was unable to look away. It warmed her from her head down to her toes.

"I might be overstepping once again, and your brother might not thank me for doing so, but I believe I have figured out the answer to your question of why I care so much about your approval." He glanced down the hall. "I believe it has a great deal to do with love."

The words were spoken quickly and in a low tone.

"I should not even acknowledge it. I know I am not the sort of gentleman you deserve. I…" He shook his head and shrugged. "I cannot even manage my own accounts. I have no right to even speak of such things until I can. And I know your brother never introduced me to you before now because my character was lacking."

"Was," Faith interrupted. "Was lacking not is lacking."

His shoulders were lifting and lowering as if breathing were difficult.

"Then I have some hope?" he asked.

Faith could appreciate how breathing while admitting one's feelings might become difficult. She pulled in a breath and nodded. "It is a venture not unworthy of consideration."

That lovely dimple appeared on his cheek.

"Might I call on you tomorrow and take you for a drive?"

Faith nodded. "I would like that." She placed her arm on his and allowed him to lead her down the hall.

Robert stood near the ballroom door, rubbing his neck and grimacing.

"Are you well?" Faith dropped Mr. Bertram's arm and hurried to her brother.

"My head is sore."

Faith raised an eyebrow. "I have only danced once." She crossed her arms.

Her brother's eyes shifted from her to Mr. Bertram and back. "Was there someone else with whom you wished to spend a half hour prancing about?"

"I do not prance. Horses prance."

"Is there?" her brother repeated.

Faith peeked up at Mr. Bertram and shook her head.

"Good. Then we must go home before my desire to play cards overtakes me."

"You are not serious," Faith replied.

"About going home, I am. Come along. Take your dear brother home so he can convalesce in peace." He turned to his friend. "Bertram, you are welcome to join us. I am certain a glass of port next to the fire will set me up quite nicely. A friend's company would not go astray."

"I will call tomorrow," Mr. Bertram said to Robert. "Your sister has given me permission to take her driving if that is acceptable to you."

Faith shook her head at the wide grin that split her brother's face as he heartily gave Mr. Bertram his blessing. Then, after a short word of parting and gathering their coats, she and Robert stepped out into the night to find their carriage.

"Best hand I ever played," he muttered to himself before chuckling softly.

Faith held his arm more tightly, leaning into his shoulder. "It seems you are not completely inept."

"Inept?" he cried.

"Thank you." Faith placed a kiss on his cheek silencing him, although the slightly smug, pleased expression remained on his face. It was enough to goad one more sharp comment from her as she entered the carriage. "Now, if only you could turn your exceptional skills of observation and stratagem towards your accounts."

Robert blew out a breath. "You are rather annoying. Did you know that?"

Faith nodded. "But I hear I am also quite wonderful."

Her brother laughed. "Yes, you are that, too," he said as the carriage door closed and they prepared to return home, both satisfied with how the evening had turned out.

Chapter 13

"I did not think we would be driving to Mr. Durward's store," Faith smiled at Tom as he stood before her, hand outstretched to see her safely from his curricle to the ground.

"I wished for you to see where I have placed my money." He hoped that she would be pleased when she saw the place. There was not much work which had happened yet, but this visit would put an image to the idea. And if she could see that image as attached to him and Gabe, then perhaps she would not associate it with Mrs. Johns. He had come up with the plan last night as he lay awake thinking about her.

"We can still drive in the park if you wish." He tucked her hand in the crook of his arm.

She shook her head. "This is perfect."

She had stopped in front of the store and was looking closely at the two bowed windows on either side of the door. She tipped her head back to look at the place where the store's name would be painted. "Have you decided on a name?"

"Not officially, but Durward and Waller will likely be what we settle on."

Her lips twitched. "Not Bertram's?"

Tom chuckled. "No. I am an investor only. I will have my own title eventually, and, therefore, I have no need of a store to bear my name."

They stepped through the door. There were men sweeping in the front while some others were working on setting shelves. A few maids were cleaning glass in cases. The floor was still dusty, but that was to be expected until everything was set and ready for the opening. Then, the wooden planks of the floor would get a good polish, and the rugs would be placed as needed.

"It will be a warehouse that carries a variety of beautiful and practical items," Tom explained. "As you can see, some of the tea caddies have already been placed on shelves. There will be ribbons and lace in one of those cases." He motioned to the display cases on his right. "Beyond that, I have very little knowledge of how everything is to be displayed, although Durward insists I must approve of it all before he allows the first customer to enter the store."

"Everyone is certainly busy," Faith said. "And it appears to be very well organized."

"Durward is particular," Tom assured her.

Gabriel Durward liked things in order. There was no danger of anything the man touched being operated in a fashion that was less than superior.

"Through here," Tom opened a door at the back of the store, "are some storerooms as well as a small parlour and accounting office. The parlour is so that the workers have a place to eat their lunch. Those stairs lead to the home above."

"Mr. Waller is claiming those accommodations, is he not?" She stood looking up the stairs to the door at the top.

"He is. I believe he will be settled into his rooms by the day after tomorrow." He watched her turn a small circle.

"It is as spacious back here as it is in the front of the store."

"But it is not as bright."

She smiled.

Was the sun able to illuminate his world as much as that smile?

"No," she agreed, "it is not bright, but it is tidy – or nearly so." She looked down at the floor which needed attention here as much as it did in the front. "But it will be completely so, I would imagine, as soon as things have settled a bit."

She was, at least, politer than Durward was in stating his expectations that the store be in exemplary shape before they opened. Durward blustered. Miss Eldridge only raised a brow and gave an expectant look. Of course, even if she had blustered, Tom would not have minded so very much for she was far prettier than Durward.

Speaking of that blustery friend, Tom opened the door to the small accounting office, where he knew Durward would likely be. "We have places to store all the important papers and such in here."

"Mr. Durward," Faith said as she stepped into the room. "It is a pleasure to see you. The store is looking quite proper."

Gabe pushed up from his spot at the desk and motioned to the one empty chair in the room. "It is progressing."

"And are you progressing?" She tapped her arm as she sat down to indicate she spoke of his injuries and not his store.

"Well enough for my mother to allow me to leave the house daily."

"Which is no easy task," Tom murmured. Mrs. Durward was a protective sort of mother. "This is Mr. Waller. Mr. Waller, Miss Eldridge."

"Ah, the financial advisor?" Waller asked with a grin.

Faith laughed. "Yes, I guess I am, but truly, Mr. Bertram does not need so much help as he thinks he does. He is a quick study."

The smile she turned on Tom was one that spoke of the truth of her words. She was proud of him. If Tom had thought he was lost to her before this precise moment, he was more than certain he was now.

"Bertram is a sharp one," Durward agreed.

"What is left to be done, aside from some cleaning and Mr. Waller taking up residence?" She leaned forward curiously looking at Durward was doing. "You have stock rooms which require filling as well as shelves and cases, and there is the matter of the sign above the door, but is everything else in order?"

Durward chuckled. "Yes. I believe all is in order. This afternoon, Waller and I are to interview a few gentlemen to begin filling the shop assistant positions." He sighed ever so slightly, but it was enough for Faith's left brow to rise in question.

"It is not always easy to allow others to do things when you are not certain they will immediately do them the way you wish," Tom explained.

Durward nodded.

"But I will be here to oversee things," Waller assured the room. "And I would like to think I can do that to Durward's exacting standards."

Tom chuckled as did his friend, Gabe.

"I am just setting up some account books so that bills can be sent in a timely fashion." Gabe looked up from where he was using a ruler to draw a line. "And so they can be paid in an equally timely fashion if the customer wishes to retain their right to acquire items before the money has been tendered. Credit is a necessary evil, but the effects of it can be curtailed by stringent parameters that do not meet with exceptions."

"Durward does not care if it is Prinny himself," Waller said, "the bill will be paid on time or credit will be discontinued until such time as the bill is paid."

"And only possibly reinstated," Durward grumbled. "Untrustworthy knaves do not deserve to be given a second go at picking my pockets."

"That is wise," Faith said.

Tom could see how she was relaxing into the chair in which she sat. Her arm rested lightly on one of the arms of the chair, and she leaned against the slightly rounded back. He was glad of it. For if she were able to relax during a discussion of credit, then there was every hope she could, and would, see this venture as a wise one. They spoke for a few moments longer about non-business-related things mostly in relation to Waller setting up his house. Then, Tom suggested it was time to be on their way.

"I will give you a tour of my lodgings as soon as it is presentable," Waller said to Faith.

"Bertram," Durward called to Tom just as he and Faith had entered the hall.

"Do you mind?" Tom asked Miss Eldridge.

She shook her head.

"I will be just a moment. You may explore while you wait."

"I will wander toward the front of the store," Faith told him before he ducked back into the office.

"You would do well to keep your financial advisor even after your accounts are in order," Gabe said as soon as Tom was entirely inside the office.

That was what his friend had called him back to tell him?

"She is charming," Waller agreed.

"And smart. What other lady would make a list of all the same things I did when first considering what must be done to get this establishment underway? I've no doubt Mansfield would tick along in a well-managed fashion with her by your side," Gabe added.

Tom shook his head. Of course, Gabe would see the practical side.

"And," Gabe smirked, "you seem rather smitten."

"Excessively," Tom agreed. "Therefore, you fellows had best get this place making money soon so that I can keep her forever."

Gabe settled back into his chair, looking very pleased. "And then we can see to Waller here."

"Waller will not refuse the assistance," Waller said, causing both Tom and Gabe to chuckle.

Tom said farewell to the gentlemen and hurried through the corridor to the front of the building to find Faith. She was standing near one of the cases, talking to a carpenter who was studying his handiwork.

"The cornice makes it look quite elegant, does it not?" she asked as Tom approached.

"Indeed, it does." He would far rather look at her than some shelf, but he turned his eyes to the top of the case. The carpenter had done an excellent job in carving some scrolls into the cornice.

"There is a groove for the plates to stand in, and then a small ledge standing up here to keep the cups from being knocked off," the carpenter explained, running his finger along the edge of the shelf.

Faith rose up on her toes to see the groove the workman had indicated. "I would not have noticed the ledge if you had not shown it to me! It is very clever."

"It is well done," Tom agreed.

She wrapped her arm around Tom's offered one and thanked the carpenter for allowing her to ask questions.

"That man was telling me," she said as they moved toward the door, "that Mr. Durward will have tea sets displayed next to the tea caddies."

"And you approve of this?" He could tell by the excitement in her voice that she did, but he asked anyway.

"I do approve. Of all of it," she answered. "The tea caddies, the glassware, the storerooms, the whole thing. But that is why you brought me here, is it not?"

Tom opened the door for her and allowed her to exit

before him. "Yes," was all he said in answer to her question.

"Why?"

Of course, a lady like Miss Eldridge would not be satisfied with a simple answer. She was curious. Tom was uncertain if he could give her a satisfactory answer, but he determined to try as he helped her into the carriage before taking his seat.

She tucked his cane between her leg and his.

"I still desire your approval." He shrugged. "And I thought it might ease your mind. I know you have said that you approve of the venture, but it was only a concept. Seeing the objects makes it more real."

"And more exciting?" Her eyes were filled with amusement.

"To me, yes." There was something about seeing a plan such as this take shape that was exhilarating.

"To me as well," she replied, moving his cane to her other side and scooting just that much closer to him.

If he shifted, which he did, his leg could touch hers. The excitement of the store that now stood behind them was nothing to the sensation of being so close to her. This venture needed to succeed and soon, for he was uncertain how long he was willing to wait to have her as his wife.

Chapter 14

"My, you look to be in fine spirits today," Mrs. Johns said when Faith entered the sitting room.

"And I see you have no crutch by your chair." Faith's answering comment was as joy-filled as her friend's greeting.

"Olivia has allowed me some freedom," Mrs. Johns replied with a chuckle.

"You must be doing well for her to allow it." Faith knew that Olivia was excessively cautious about her mother's recovery, which according to Faith was as it ought to be.

"Indeed, I am. Soon enough I will be able to walk to the store and purchase my own supplies." She tied off what she had been stitching and snipped the thread.

Faith gathered some work from the basket. Her heart sank as she did so. Mrs. John's foot might heal, and her hand might not ache as much as it did, but this basket of sewing would always be her lot. There would never be an end to this. Her needs would demand it.

"You needn't attempt to create lines before your time."

Faith lifted startled eyes to Mrs. John. She had no idea what such a comment meant.

"There was a deep line between your eyebrows just now. What troubles you?"

Faith shook her head. "It was nothing. Just a thought." She did not wish to discuss money or the lack of it with her friend's mother.

"You do not need to sew," Mrs. Johns said. "My fingers are working quite well these days."

Again, Faith shook her head. "It is not that. I do not mind sewing. I never have."

Mrs. Johns placed her work on the table and took off the spectacles she used to do close work. "Then what is it? I will not be put off."

Faith sat down, threaded her needle, and considered how she would answer such a direct demand. When she was ready to begin sewing, she asked, "Do you mind sewing?"

"I never have – until now." Mrs. Johns lifted the article of clothing she had been mending. "It is not as pleasant to do it so often, or for people whom you do not know and love." She expelled a great breath. "However, I find that imagining the pleasure of some gentleman or lady when they get their clothing delivered to them in fine repair, makes the task less odious." She tipped her head and smiled at Faith. "And I am putting aside a few pence as

I can so that I might one day be able to give it to you to invest for me."

"You are?" Faith's needle stilled. She had not thought that her friends might ever have enough to invest, but it would be an excellent thing for them to do. There just might actually be an end to all this sewing if money could be put to work properly. If only Mrs. Johns had been left more by her husband, then they might already be working their way out of workbaskets and music lessons and back towards what they had always known.

"I am not without a quick mind, my dear. I did run an estate and kept it as solvent as I could despite my husband's weaknesses." She sighed. "I miss him – towering merchant accounts and all. We loved each other dearly. He forgave me my weaknesses, and I forgave him his – as long as his weakness did not involve the keeping of a mistress – that was my one stipulation. A woman who can abide a husband who wanders from bed to bed is beyond my ability to comprehend, even if I do know there are many who do put up with such things."

"If a woman could provide for herself..." Faith did not finish the statement.

"Perhaps one day all young ladies will be as learned as you are in the workings of percents and such."

"Perhaps," Faith agreed.

"Now that I have discovered what caused your frown, I should like to discover what was the source of your smile before you began to worry for *my* future." Mrs. Johns rose and limped to where the workbaskets were laid out. She placed her finished garment in the basket on the left before taking a new project from the basket on the right. "Does it have anything to do with your young man?"

Her young man. Those were very pleasant words to hear, for Mr. Bertram – Tom, she rolled his name around her mouth silently – was indeed hers. He had only to earn back his losses, and then he would offer for her. He had said nearly those exact words on three occasions.

"Tell me about how wonderful he is," Mrs. John's prodded. "I wish to hear all about your good fortune in finding a gentleman who loves you as you deserve."

"You may not start any discussion of Mr. Bertram without me," Olivia said from the door. "I have only to go up to my room for a moment."

"We will wait," her mother assured her. "But be quick," she called after her. "Olivia might have a fourth student," Mrs. Johns said to Faith. "Soon, she shall have one for every day of the week, and then more of my sewing money can be set aside."

"That is excellent."

Mrs. Johns raised an eyebrow and gave Faith a pointed look. "You do not sound as happy as you should be."

"She should be singing at musicales in music rooms not teaching in one." The fact that Olivia could not participate in any of the activities where she might find a husband was one of the things that caused Faith to feel a trifle guilty for having found a happy future with Mr. Bertram.

"Someone will find her. She is too beautiful to be ignored for long." Mrs. Johns assured Faith. "Three of the possible four young ladies who come for lessons have brothers who escort them to our door – unmarried brothers." She pressed her lips together quickly as Olivia entered.

"Now, you may tell us all about Mr. Bertram," Olivia said. "You have not been to see us in days, and the last we heard you had danced with him at a ball and were going to go driving with him."

Faith had insisted that Robert allow her to spend a few hours with Olivia and her mother after that ball where her brother had played matchmaker. He had sent a note to Mr. Bertram telling him to call an hour later than was normal, and Mr. Bertram had not grumbled one bit about being put off for an hour.

"He took me to see the store that he is helping finance." She put her sewing aside while she spoke. "It was in the process of being made ready. We will have to go there together when it is opened. It shall be quite a sought-after place, I can tell you that. I was impressed by the plans and with the work that had been done when I saw it. Mr. Bertram was correct about Mr. Durward never doing anything which is not excellent. I quite approve of Mr. Durward. He was drawing up ledgers when we were there, and he has some very firm beliefs about credit not being abused." She looked down at her empty lap.

"You may say whatever it is you are thinking," Mrs. Johns encouraged. "I know my husband's weaknesses. I shall not faint away to hear them mentioned."

"Are you certain?" Faith asked quietly.

"I am positive," Mrs. Johns said.

Faith blew out a breath. "He will not extend credit to anyone who has not settled accounts within a specified amount of time, so his store will not contribute to someone needing to take in sewing to keep herself." She smiled apologetically at Mrs. Johns.

"I think that is a very good thing," Olivia said.

"As do I," Mrs. Johns agreed, reaching over to grasp Faith's hand. "You are so caring, my dear. So caring."

Faith blinked against the tears in her eyes. "I wish I could do more for you."

"And I would not allow you. You do enough as it is. Dressing like a maid to come visit us and spend your time sewing things for which you will not receive a cent – that is enough."

"It does not feel like enough," Faith admitted. She felt so guilty for her own good fortune – for having a father who saw to finances as he should and for a brother who was caring enough to be badgered into learning to behave properly.

"Well, it is," Olivia said. "Of course, when you are Lady

Bertram, I should not be opposed to being asked to visit you."

"Olivia!" her mother scolded.

Faith laughed. "You could not keep me from asking for such a thing, and," her cheeks flushed, "I am certain Mr. Bertram would be willing to allow me to invite you both."

"I am so pleased for you!" Olivia cried. "When will you allow us to meet... Does he know you are here?" She rose from her chair and went to the window. "For it seems as if he wishes to stop here."

"Whatever do you mean?" Faith joined her friend at the window just as Tom removed his hat and ran a hand through his hair. Something was wrong.

"I must speak to him," she said, moving quickly to the door of the sitting room.

"Invite him in," Mrs. Johns called after her. "You can speak in the music room."

"Thank you," Faith said from the doorway before rushing to open the front door and call to Mr. Bertram before he rode away.

"Mr. Bertram!" She waved to him from the step, her heart sinking as she took in his expression when he turned her direction. There was a deep furrow between his eyes and a sad downward turn to his mouth.

"Come in," she said when he rode over to her.

"I cannot," he turned and looked up the street and then back at her as if he was lost.

"Please, come in and tell me what has happened. Please." She held her breath as he deliberated if he should do as she asked or not. Finally, he swung down from his horse, and tying it up, entered the Johns' home.

"In here." She motioned to the music room.

He paused at the door. "I should greet the ladies of the house. It is only proper."

Faith was not at all certain that he was in any condition to greet anyone, but she acquiesced and led him into the sitting room. "Mrs. Johns, Miss Johns," she said, "this is Mr. Bertram."

Olivia and her mother both rose and curtseyed.

"It is good to meet you," Mrs. Johns said, "but, forgive me, you do not look well, sir. Is there anything we can get you for your relief?"

"A glass of wine," Olivia offered.

"No, indeed, ma'am. I thank you, but I shall be well as soon as...well..." he shrugged. "I do not actually know when I will be well. I have had some dreadful news." He looked at Faith, and she thought he might cry because his eyes were glistening.

"Then do not let us keep you from doing what needs to be done," Mrs. Johns said. "I do hope you will call on us when things are in a better state for you."

He nodded and, giving a small bow, ducked out of the room and crossed to the music room where he paced the small room for a moment before turning to Faith. He opened his mouth to speak and closed it again before dropping into a chair and saying, "I may be Sir Thomas before the end of the week."

Faith's hand flew to her heart. The poor man! No wonder he looked lost.

"There was a fire." He shook his head. "A candle tipped over. One wing of the house is in need of repair."

"And your father?"

"He was injured in the task of putting out the flames. His shirtsleeve...." He pressed his lips together and shook his head.

"He was burned?"

Mr. Bertram nodded and blew out a breath. "Mother has told me not to rush excessively in returning home, but I will leave tomorrow." Again, he shook his head. "After I see Durward," he added in a whisper. "I would see him today, but he is overseeing the arrival of a shipment of goods. Mansfield will need the money. I cannot leave my home in ruins to pursue our venture." He rose. "Mr. Gardiner may be willing to join them, or perhaps his nephew Mr. Darcy would like to invest with them." He turned his hat in his hands. "Someone will take my place."

"Oh, Tom," Faith whispered.

He did not lift his eyes from studying the hat in his hands. "I cannot marry – not now. Not for some time. I will understand if you cannot wait. I do not know how long it will take to set things to right at Mansfield, but I cannot ask you to be my wife when things are as they are. I will not put you in danger of..." He looked up and around the room. "Of this. I would never wish to even have you worry that this might be your lot because I was foolish in my youth and wasted my inheritance."

He took the few steps necessary to close the gap between them. A tear slid down his cheek when he placed his hand on her cheek. "I will always love you," he whispered.

"And I, you," she pressed her cheek into his hand, desperately wanting him to understand that she would be his no matter the circumstances.

He shook his head. "No." He kissed her forehead. "Find another. Do not waste your life waiting for me." He kissed her forehead once again, and then hurried from the room.

Chapter 15

The miles ticked by much more slowly than normal as Tom sat inside his carriage attempting to occupy his mind with something worthwhile instead of either disappointment or sorrow. He had managed to sleep for part of the trip – likely because he had not slept at all last night. He had paced and paced.

He leaned his head back and blew a breath at the ceiling of the vehicle. Meeting with Durward had not been easy. A man did not like to feel his failure or see it in the sad smile of his friend. Of course, Durward understood the need for Tom to withdraw from the offer.

"Only if a replacement can be found," Tom said to the emptiness of the carriage. Part of him wished for Durward to have success straightaway in finding another partner, and part of him – the part that wanted so badly to succeed in a venture he had chosen – wanted it to be an impossible thing to replace him. But he knew that he was not irreplaceable. Funds could be found elsewhere. There had to be at least one other investor of fine character of whom Durward would approve.

He closed his eyes and imagined a fair face and sunset hair. If only he had not been so foolish in his past. If only he had not wasted so much money. If only he had succeeded in his venture with Durward and been able to marry Miss Eldridge before he was to be faced with the possibility of claiming his inheritance. That was likely the part of the whole ordeal that hurt the most.

He did not know exactly what he would find at Mansfield when he arrived, but he knew it would not be anything which would make him financially sound enough to offer for Faith. She had seen the devastation of a mismanaged estate. *He* had seen it in the few moments it had taken him to greet Mrs. and Miss Johns. He could not ask her to put herself in a place that would cause her worry – not even for a few years.

He wished with all his heart that he could just throw off this new responsible Tom and act impulsively as he used to do. Then, he would be able to reason himself into accepting that things were not as bad as they seemed. It would not be too much to ask her to marry him. Nor was it necessary to repay what was lost. A fire was not something for which someone could plan. It was an act of God providing him with a reason to stop running after repaying his debts.

He shook his head and laughed sadly. He could see those deep blue eyes of his angel narrowing as her lips pursed and her arms folded across her lovely chest. And he knew that, while a fire could not be foreseen and disasters did occur, a gentleman must have laid aside something to assist in such times. He had heard her say something very like that to Robert on more than one occasion during a financial meeting.

He sighed and looked out the window just as Mansfield came into sight. There were boarded up windows in the damaged wing, but other than that, there was no evidence of fire from the outside. Perhaps the cost of repairs would be less than what he expected.

Sadly, when he finally arrived, and, after greeting his mother, had been shown the destruction left by the fire, he knew that while the shell of the wing was intact, the interior would all need to be rebuilt. There were too many damaged beams. A house would not stand the test of time if its structure were merely patched up to appear to be proper. His lips curled upward slightly. Miss Eldridge would approve of such a thought.

Tom stood at the entrance to the damaged wing and shook his head.

"It is overwhelming, is it not?" his younger brother, Edmund, asked.

Tom nodded. "I feel gutted." He blew out a breath and gathered his resolve. "But, we shall see it healed eventually. I will set upon creating a plan as soon as I have seen Father. Will you join me?"

"In seeing Father?" Edmund asked as they began walking toward the staircase which would lead them to the floor upon which the family quarters were located.

"Yes, that and in creating a plan. You always were better with numbers than I was, and you always knew what was best to do."

Edmund laughed. "Not always. I nearly married Miss Crawford."

"Well, yes, there is that," Tom replied with a grin. "She is betrothed, by the way."

"Is she, indeed?" There was no little amount of surprise in his brother's tone. "I mean, I never expected she would not marry, but..." He shrugged. "I do not know what I thought actually."

"I would imagine you thought very little about a woman who is not your wife." How long had it been since he and Edmund had actually spoken so easily about anything?

"This is true," Edmund agreed. "Fanny is..." His voice trailed off, and he shook his head.

"So much more than you could have imagined finding?"

Edmund paused on the step just before the landing and looked up at his older brother in surprise. "Yes, but how do you know that?"

Tom shrugged and turned away from him.

"Have you found a lady to marry?" Edmund asked as he hurried to catch up to his brother.

Tom paused with his hand on the doorknob to his father's room. "I thought I had."

Edmund pushed at Tom's shoulder attempting to turn Tom to face him. "What happened?"

Tom drew and released two breaths before he found the words that he thought he could say with any amount of calm. "Let me see Father first."

"Of course," Edmund replied just as Tom knew he would. Edmund was far too obliging at times, although at present Tom was happy for that particular character trait.

"You know," Edmund continued, "I am not without some experience in thinking I was in love only to discover I was not."

Tom held the door open and was just about to enter. "No," he said softly, "you are not. However, I have not found myself to have thought I was in love." Looking into the room, he could just see the end of his father's bed. "I love her very dearly," he said to Edmund and then added, "but first we must see father."

His father attempted to smile when Tom approached the bed.

"It is good to see you, my son," Sir Thomas said in a voice that did not entirely sound like his father. It was much more feeble sounding than Tom had ever heard. Even when his father had been ill for a time in Antigua, he had not sounded as weak as he did now.

Tom swallowed the sorrow he felt at such a revelation

and rested a hand on his father's leg. He would have grasped his hand, but it was bandaged as was his chest. A small bit of scorched skin showed on the left side of his father's neck. A bottle of laudanum stood on the table beside the bed next to a decanter of wine. The pain his father was in must be immense.

"You have done well," his father continued. "I was pleased to read your last report."

"Thank you, but we do not need to speak of finances at present. You should rest."

His father grimaced as he shook his head slightly. "No, we must talk while I still can. I am not unaware that these injuries might claim me even if Fanny assures me they will not. She is such a sweet girl, you know."

"I have no doubt she is," Tom answered. "She always was when she was young."

"I wish I had noticed it when she was a girl," his father stared at the ceiling above him. "There is a lot that I wish I had done but did not."

"And there is a lot that I have done which I wish I had not," Tom said solemnly.

"Speaking of which," his father said, "the money I had given you for your purposes..."

"I have spoken to Durward, and the money should be available to me shortly to put toward repairs."

"Durward?" Edmund asked.

"The fellow he was going into business with," their

father replied before turning his eyes toward Tom. "I am sorry, son."

"Not as much as I am," Tom answered honestly.

"It is not easy to step away from a business arrangement," his father said.

Tom shook his head. "It was more than that." He rose and paced to the window. "Durward is a friend, a very good friend – perhaps the best I have ever had." He looked at Edmund. "He is marrying Miss Crawford."

Edmund's eyes grew wide.

"She has changed. Thanks in no small part to Durward's influence, although I do suppose her brother's cutting her off had something to do with it as well."

"Crawford cut off his sister?" their father asked.

"You must tell us that tale," Edmund said.

Tom brought a chair over to sit next to Edmund and his father and shared with them all of what he knew about both Crawfords' change of heart. The story, of course, astonished his audience.

"And this Durward is marrying Miss Crawford?" Edmund repeated. "And she has changed so much?"

Tom nodded, his brow furrowing. "You are not regretting your decision to part ways with her, are you?"

Edmund snapped from his contemplation. "No, never!" he cried. "I was only pondering how wrong I was in thinking she would always be as she always was."

"She likely would have been, had it not been for your

rejection of her." His younger brother was too agreeable. Edmund never would have provided the resistance Miss Crawford would have needed to mend her ways. "You are not a reformer, Edmund. You are much too kind."

"Soft, you mean," Edmund grumbled.

Tom shook his head. "I do not mean soft. I mean kind. I know how stubborn you can be. You are not soft."

"Pliable then," Edmund amended.

Once again, Tom shook his head. "Only because you are kind and generous and excessively forgiving. And those are all qualities for which I am grateful since my focus was on myself instead of anyone else for so long. You have forgiven me for my foolishness, have you not?"

"Of course," Edmund replied without so much as a moment's pause.

"You do not need to repay your debt," their father interrupted.

"No," Tom answered, "I owe it to both my present and my future family." Even if it would cost him dearly. However, pain or no pain, he would not be the man he had been. He would face his responsibilities now as he should have then.

Chapter 16

"You gave her up for this?" Edmund looked aghast as he motioned toward the shelves behind their father's desk the following morning.

As much as Tom had wanted to immediately begin looking at account books and making plans, his mother had insisted that he not lock himself away in his father's study. That had, of course, meant that Edmund had not been able to hear about Miss Eldridge until now.

Tom nodded in answer to his brother's question. Was that not what he had just said?

"You found a lady whom you love, but you gave her up to rebuild part of the house?"

It was as if his brother had become deficient in his ability to grasp a topic.

"Not just to rebuild that part of the house. There is also the need to repay what I lost. Mansfield would be in a much better state and able to weather this disaster far more easily if that money had never been lost."

Edmund who had been standing looking out the window while Tom told him about Faith, came around the desk and dropped into a chair. "You cannot just toss love away."

"I am not –" Tom stopped, his brow furrowing. Was he throwing something precious away for something of far less worth? He would not question his actions if someone – nearly anyone – else doubted him. But this was Edmund. Edmund did not value things as cheaply as some did. "Do you think I am? Have I chosen wrongly?"

"A heart is far more valuable than a well-arranged pile of bricks and mortar," Edmund replied with a grin. "However, do not tell Father I said that. He would likely disagree. You know how Mansfield has been his everything."

Tom leaned back in his chair, ignoring the account book before him. Edmund was correct. To their father, education, the proper allotment of finances, correct connections, marrying properly, and all the other "proprieties" associated with an estate and making one's mark on wealthy society had outshone warmth and... Tom sighed. Love. It was not as if Tom had considered himself unloved when he was growing up, but he had to admit there had always been a longing for something more than a lecture on impropriety or a short *well-done* on which to hang his hopes of approval.

He shook his head. "I cannot ask her to take on an estate that is not fully sorted. You do not understand. I need for her to feel secure."

"Is Mansfield on the brink of ruin?" Edmund asked.

"No, but it is facing a large financial burden. Rebuilding will not be quick or inexpensive."

Edmund tipped his head and studied his older brother for a moment. "I cannot imagine my life without Fanny, Tom. I would not care what sort of house I had or what food was on my table if I did not have her by my side. What good is a beautiful manor house if it is empty and cold from lack of love?" He shrugged. "Do not pretend to not know what that might feel like. We do. Father did his best, but even he has admitted his errors. Being the master of Mansfield does not mean becoming like Father."

Become like his father? The idea was laughable, was it not?

It was most certainly frightening. Tom and his father were nothing alike. He had always been miserable attempting to win his father's approval. There was no way he was going to consign his life to such misery willingly. But...

"How do I avoid such a thing and yet secure my legacy?"

"What does Mansfield need to function as a proper estate? Does it need all it holds? Are there some things for which the loss of those holding would be of greater benefit to the estate than retaining them?" Edmund's lips tipped up. "The living which was sold was not necessary for the estate to function. That is why Father sold it."

"But it was to be yours," Tom protested.

"And it is."

"But it might not have been."

Edmund shook his head. "Eventually, it would have been mine. Dr. Grant was not the sort of fellow to live forever." He lifted his eyebrows and gave Tom a meaningful look. "Father was no fool. He did not sell it to someone who was young and would likely live as long as I would."

Tom had never considered that before.

"Why do you think I was so complacent about the sale?"

"Because you are Edmund," Tom said with a shrug.

His brother laughed. "I am certain that was part of it, but I knew that with time I would receive that living."

A great heavy wave of emotion settled on Tom's shoulders. "I have spent years feeling that error most grievously I can assure you." He shook his head. "You really expected to receive it eventually?"

Edmund nodded. "So, you see, your debt is not as great as you imagined. Mansfield has survived quite well." He drew a breath. "If I were to advise you in any way related to the removal of properties from Mansfield, I would suggest looking at those which are the furthest removed from where we are sitting right now."

Was his brother suggesting what Tom thought he was suggesting?

"This venture you were going to be part of," Edmund continued, "do you think it has the potential to replace some or all of the income from the Antiqua property?"

Edmund *was* suggesting what Tom thought he was suggesting, and the thought brought a smile to Tom's face. He had despised nearly every moment of his time in Antiqua.

"I am not certain if it would..." His voice trailed off as he thought about the two people who would most likely be able to help him decipher the answer. Both were in town. One was a cunning businessman and the other was a daring young woman who claimed to abhor risk.

He would have to write to Durward immediately. Hopefully, he had not already found an investor. He pulled out a sheet of paper and putting the account book aside, prepared to write his letter. After this letter, he would need to write a second one to –

"Come," he called to whoever had rapped on the door.

"You have callers, sir," the butler said. "Are you home?"

"I am." Tom was curious as to who would be calling on him. There were few who knew he was at home.

The butler disappeared for a moment before returning with Tom's guests.

"Miss Eldridge?" Tom cried, rising quickly from his chair.

"Is she?" Edmund whispered.

Tom nodded, happiness suffusing his features.

Faith moved toward the desk. "Mr. Durward had some news he knew you would wish to hear, and Robert," she motioned to her brother, "was good enough to offer to accompany me in delivering Mr. Durward's message."

"I did not offer," Robert grumbled. "I was given no

choice." He raised a brow and glared at his sister. "I thought it would be very bad form to arrive unannounced at a home where things were in disarray."

"No, no," Tom protested. "I am happy to see you both. In fact, I was just about to write to Durward and then you, Robert." He shook his head. "Forgive me. Miss Eldridge, Robert, this is my brother, Edmund."

Edmund was looking at Faith very curiously. "Do I know you?"

Faith pressed her lips together and blushed.

"You do," Tom answered for her. "She cared for me when I was ill and you came to get me."

Edmund shook his head. "No, that was a servant girl." His face scrunched. "Her name escapes me just now."

"Eliza?" Faith offered.

"Yes, yes, that was it!"

"I am she. I disguised myself as a maid since it is not the thing to do for a young lady to care for a gentleman." She shrugged. "It was necessary."

Edmund looked from Faith to his brother and back before he seemed able to respond to such a revelation. "I thank you for saving my brother."

"How could I not?" Faith said with a smile before growing serious and adding, "You will not tell anyone will you?"

"My wife," he answered. "Fanny will be delighted to meet the lady who saved our Tom. I will tell no one else."

"Edmund is a man of his word. He always has been. Even when we were boys," Tom inserted. "And Fanny is the same. Your secret is safe."

Faith's smile returned. "That is excellent, and I am certain you will find Mr. Durward's news to be as pleasing as I find the fact that my impropriety will not be spread hither and yon." She placed some papers on the desk and took a seat before it, waiting expectantly until Tom reclaimed his place.

"You did not use your cane," she scolded when he winced. "You will not improve if you do not take care."

"Is that the message from Durward's mother?" He teased, causing her to roll her eyes.

"No, it is my own," she retorted.

"My sister is demanding," Robert whispered to Edmund.

"I am not," Faith argued.

Robert merely lifted a skeptical brow in response.

"Oh, very well, I can be, but only when it is necessary." She grinned at her brother.

To Tom, there seemed to be a great many things which Miss Eldridge excused as necessary of which she might not otherwise approve.

"She is always well-meaning," Robert added.

"That she is," Tom agreed.

"Most times," Faith admitted before leaning toward Edmund and adding, "there are times, however, when it is absolutely necessary to provoke one's brother. Do you not agree?"

Edmund chuckled. "Indeed, Miss Eldridge, I think I must agree."

Tom shook his head. Miss Eldridge would do very well as a part of this family. After he heard Durward's news, perhaps he could speak to the lady in private and retract his suggestion that she not wait for him.

"I went to see Mr. Clarke yesterday." She smoothed the top piece of paper in the pile of four or five that she had placed on the desk. "And then, I visited Mr. Durward and Mr. Waller."

Tom wondered if she had changed from her breeches to her dress.

"After a stop at home," Robert said with a glare at Tom. It was as if the fellow could read Tom's thoughts.

Faith pulled a paper from the pile. "It seems Mr. Durward has taken on a new partner for his venture."

Tom's breath hitched. He was too late. He had been replaced and in only a day. His heart sank.

"And it seems that they have agreed on a name for their store," Faith continued.

"Have they?" Tom was not certain he wished to know anything more about the store at this moment.

Faith handed him the paper she held as she spoke. "They are thinking of calling it Durward, Waller, and Eldridge."

Tom's mouth dropped open, and he looked from the paper he held to Robert. Had Robert taken his place?

Robert shook his head and pointed to his sister, who was looking down at her hands.

"Unless, of course, you would prefer it to be Durward, Waller, and Bertram." She lifted her eyes to his. "It was my money, but if you read that paper, you will see it was done in your name."

Tom's eyes returned to the document he held. It was as she had said. His money was to be released to him and another sum, one that was slightly higher than what Tom had invested, was to be added to the venture in his name.

"We only need your signature," she added.

He looked at her and shook his head. How could he allow her to do this?

"You will sign it," she said. "Mr. Durward insists."

Robert coughed to cover a chuckle.

Tom knew very well that Durward was only insisting at Miss Eldridge's behest.

"It is necessary," she added before pulling another sheet out from her pile. "I have seen your numbers as you know."

"You have?" Edmund interjected.

"She has been advising me on financial matters," Tom explained to his startled and somewhat confused brother.

"I know you said I should not wait for you to get things settled here at Mansfield, but I disagree." Her cheeks were flushed as she handed him the folded paper she held. "I have been doing some thinking, you see, and have come to the conclusion that there are times when taking a risk is... well... It is necessary." She blinked against the tears he could see glistening in her eyes.

Tom glanced at his brother and nodded toward the door. Thankfully, Edmund understood and rose to leave. Robert moved to follow.

"Do you know about this?" Tom asked, lifting the missive he held in his hand.

Robert nodded. "It is about time she found a reason to throw caution to the wind."

Tom waited until the door had closed behind Robert. Then, he rose and took the seat next to Faith in front of his desk.

"It is all I have. There is no more." She shrugged. "But what good does it do me if it comes at the cost of my heart? If you will have me, my dowry could do a great deal for Mansfield. It could secure your legacy. That is what you have wished to do, is it not?"

She did not need to ask him twice. He did not need the inducement of her fortune to wish to marry her, even if she had included it below her question on that missive. He picked up a pen and jotted a quick, *gladly* under her *marry me* before crossing out the twenty thousand pounds. Then, he handed the paper back to her.

"I will not marry you for your money," he said.

"You cannot marry me without taking it," she retorted, a smile spreading across her face as she read his response on the paper.

"Then, I will have to make peace with accepting it, but I want you to know that I wish to marry you only because I love you." He took the paper from her and placed it on the desk so that he could hold her hands and draw her to her feet and into his embrace. "I think we will let the store bear your name so that you can claim a new name – mine." He pulled back and looked down at her. "My angel. You have saved me more than once. I would be lost without you. You truly wish to be my wife?"

"With all my heart," she replied.

Tom, of course, sealed the agreement as any good gentleman would – with a kiss that was filled with longing as well as the peace that comes when a heart has found its safe haven. And as his hands held her close delighting in the softness of her form while her lips parted to allow him to deepen the kiss and her hands found their way first to wind around his neck and then to tangle in his hair, Tom knew that his legacy would be secure. However, it would not only be a legacy of land and wealth as he had expected. It would be something far greater, for his would be a legacy of the heart.

Before You Go

If you enjoyed this book, be sure to let others know by leaving a review.

~*~*~

Want to know when the next book in this series will be available?

You can always know what's new with my books by subscribing to my mailing list.

(There will, of course, be a thank you gift for joining because I think my readers are awesome!)

Book News from Leenie Brown

(bit.ly/LeenieBBookNews)

~*~*~

Turn the page to read an excerpt of another one of Leenie's books

His Beautiful Bea Excerpt

[If you enjoy books based on *Mansfield Park*, then you might like *His Beautiful Bea*, an original sweet Regency romance, written with intentional nods to *Mansfield Park*, and the first book in my *Touches of Austen Collection*. In this book, Graeme Clayton attempts to help his neighbour Beatrice Tierney capture the heart of his younger brother, but things don't quite go according to plan.]

CHAPTER 1

Beatrice Tierney blew out a breath and settled back against a tree in Stratsbury Park's garden, attempting to find a comfortable position in which to read. The weather was warm, but not unbearably so, and the shade cast by the sprawling canopy overhead provided a pleasant respite from the rays of the sun. A breeze occasionally fluttered the hem of her skirt and attempted to turn the pages of her book. All in all, it would be a perfect summer day, were it not for her cousins, Felicity and Grace Love. Bea's lips twitched with displeasure as she turned her attention back to the page she had read twice already.

She brushed away a fly that was meandering a path across the words she was attempting to decipher just as a long shadow crossed the page, causing her to look up to see its source.

"Is it a difficult passage?" Graeme Clayton stood looking down at her. He chuckled as her lips puckered into a deeper scowl. He knew very well that Bea was not short on intelligence. She might be quiet and verging on the edge of overly reserved and gentle, but it was not due to lack of intellect. In fact, when she did open her mouth and speak on any subject, her comments were often impressively well-thought-out. He knew that she studied things — mulling them over and over, assessing them from every possible angle, and then, and only then, having decided she had a good grasp of her ideas, her thoughts on a matter might be shared. Equally as often as not, however, she would merely smile softly, raise a brow, and remain silent. It perplexed him how she could keep her opinions to herself so often. He had a devil of a time keeping his tongue from saying exactly what was in his head.

Today, for the past twenty minutes, he had been observing her as she attempted to read and not watch his younger brother, Everett, and her cousin Felicity. She had sighed and shaken her head often, her lips had pursed, her brows had furrowed, and the pages of her book had not flipped in all that time. She was contemplating something, and he was rather certain he knew what it was.

Bea had always followed his brother around with a particular look on her face that spoke of her adoration of him. It was not an obvious expression. It was a particular softness in her eyes and the tipping up ever so slightly of the corners of her mouth.

He took a seat next to her on the ground and, giving her shoulder a nudge with his, repeated his question, earning him a very pretty scowl. However, as quickly as the scowl had formed on her lips, it melted away into the pleasant expression she wore in company when she would rather be elsewhere but did not wish to offend.

She was about to deny there was any issue at all — much as she always did. Others were permitted to be displeased and out of sorts, but Bea never allowed herself to be so — at least, not in company. One had to look for more subtle clues as to how Bea was really feeling, but that was just one thing what made her uniquely his Bea.

"No," she began her denial, just as he had predicted in his mind that she would, "the passage is not difficult. I was just distracted by the excellence of the weather."

Graeme, who was not content to let the situation pass so neatly, snatched her book out of her hands. It might be entirely possible to provoke her into revealing the truth of what he suspected. "Your distraction has nothing to do with my brother?" he asked as he snapped the book closed on her marker. Ah, there was her look of panic — a slight widening of the eyes and a sharp, though quiet, inhale of breath. He had obviously hit on the very thing which she was valiantly attempting to conceal.

Though they were only neighbours, Bea and her brother, Maxwell, had spent so many hours in company with Graeme and Everett that Graeme felt he knew the Tierney siblings almost as well as he knew his own brother. Well, "only neighbours" was perhaps not the most accurate way to describe who the Tierneys were to the Claytons.

Captain Tierney and Sir William Clayton had been friends since childhood, and when the captain had come into some money — enough to buy a small estate for his family — he had settled on Heathcote which was not more than four miles distance from the west of Stratsbury Park. And in such a manner had begun a closer friendship between their families. They spent many a day and evening in one another's company during that first month after the Tierneys' arrival at Heathcote.

And then had come the day when Captain Tierney had been required to return to his ship. He had called on his friend Sir Herbert the evening before and extracted a promise to care for Mrs. Tierney and his children if something unfortunate should befall him. As fate would have it, the unfortunate did befall the captain, and he had never returned from sea.

Bea had borne the news with far more fortitude than Graeme had expected to find in one so young and female. It was then that he had taken a greater liking to her. She was not like the silly girls he had met over the years. She was unique in her quiet strength and resolve. And so very unlike himself that he found himself compelled to attempt an understanding of such a person. His reward had been a comfortable friendship that allowed him access to the Beatrice others looking on would likely not suspect existed.

He nudged her shoulder again. "I do not believe it was the weather disturbing your reading," he whispered. "Are you positive your distraction has nothing to do with my brother?"

Bea shrugged.

Seeing he was not likely to get more of a reply from Bea than that, Graeme switched tactics and pressed on. "Miss Love is very pretty. How old is she now?"

Bea heaved a sigh. "Felicity is nineteen, just as I am, and Grace is seventeen."

"Are they both out?" he asked, moving her book away from the hand that attempted to reclaim it. He was not leaving this spot today without finding out if his suspicions about Bea's feelings for his brother were correct.

"Yes," Bea's lips stretched into a thin smile. "I have been regaled with the delights of the season several times since their arrival a fortnight ago."

Graeme shifted, placing the book on the grass next to him and stretching out his legs.

"Will you be going to town this next season? I could make a good number of introductions for you, and even with your modest dowry, I believe, we could find you a suitable husband."

He had not even finished speaking before her head was shaking back and forth.

"You will not go? I thought Max said he had put aside enough to give you a bit of a season."

"I do not wish to go. I have no desire to endure the crushes about which my cousins have told me. I prefer our small assemblies here."

"I imagine it will be harder to find a gentleman worthy of you here, but I have not been to an assembly in some time. Perhaps there is someone who has already captured your heart?" He tipped his head and studied her face carefully, looking for any indication that there might be a gentleman she already preferred.

The signs he sought were there — the slight blush on her cheek and the lowering of her eyes — but he chose to ignore them and continued on. "There is always Bath. I would assume the crowds are not so great as in London, and Mother has been forever begging father to take her there. I am certain she would enjoy taking you along. She does enjoy your company."

Bea ran a finger absent-mindedly along the chain that

held a pendant Graeme knew contained a lock of her father's hair. Between that action and the way she had pulled the corner of her bottom lip between her teeth, he knew she was considering the possibility of going to Bath. However, as fascinating as that fact was, it did not help him discern her feelings about his brother. So, he circled around to Everett once again. "Everett is planning one last go of the season before he takes up his position."

Bea nodded. "I know."

There was an interesting sadness to her tone. "Unless, of course, he finds a lady before then. Perhaps Miss Love will be capable of finally snaring him."

There it was — a small, sad, fleeting frown. It was true. Beatrice Tierney was in love with his brother — the fortunate clod. Hailed as the more studious of the two Clayton brothers, what Everett possessed in the ability to apply himself to his studies and excel, he lacked in his capacity to see the subtly obvious before him. However, Graeme would contemplate how his brother could have missed recognizing Bea's preference for him later. Right now, he needed to make Bea smile.

"Many have tried to bring him up to snuff, you know, but none have succeeded. He is a handsome devil — much like his older brother."

Bea chuckled. "He is, at least, more humble than his brother," she chided.

"So, you do not deny that the Clayton brothers are handsome?" Graeme teased.

Bea rolled her eyes. "I am not blind," she said with a light swat to Graeme's arm.

"Neither am I," Graeme retorted.

Bea's brows furrowed in confusion.

"I am not speaking of being blind to my own comeliness," he smiled at her. "For I assure you that I know precisely how fetching I look." He winked and then chuckled as she once again rolled her eyes. It was always a joy to provoke her just enough to elicit a small response such as he had just received.

"I see many things clearly. For instance, I can see that Miss Love and Miss Grace are attractive and well-skilled in all the arts required to capture a husband." He shrugged. "There are many such ladies in London, who, if they wish a desired outcome, will do their best to achieve it no matter the ploys and scheming necessary."

He nodded in response to her wide-eyed questioning look. "A fellow has to tread carefully. However, that is not all I see clearly."

"It is not?"

"No, it is not." He crossed his arms and leaned against the trunk of the tree, his shoulder brushing against hers, and his arm wishing to wrap around her and pull her close to his side as he had done when she was just a girl. However, she was no longer a mere child, and he was not her brother, so unless he wished to get scolded and have her dash away, neither of which would assist his cause, he refrained.

"I also see the way you look at my brother, and frankly, he is a fool to ignore you. I would not ignore a lady of beauty and good character such as yourself if she was to look at me so longingly." He pressed his lips together to keep from chuckling at the quick breath she drew. He had shocked her just as he had planned.

"I do no such thing," Bea refuted weakly.

"Lying does not become you, my beautiful Bea."

"Do not call me that. I am not beautiful."

He peeked over at her. Her cheeks were aflame as he knew they would be. "My dear, if there is one thing I know, it is beautiful women, and you are definitely beautiful – beguiling, even, when you blush so prettily." He reached out a hand and grabbed her arm to prevent her from jumping to her feet and running away. Bea did not like compliments of her person or actions. She preferred to fade into the background — to act without recognition or praise, qualities that would serve a parson's wife well, but also qualities that made it easy for a numbskull, soon-to-be parson, like his brother to overlook her.

"Now," he said, holding her arm firmly as she tried to pull it out of his grasp, "as I have said, I am of the belief that my brother is an idiot and Miss Love is a grasping...," he cleared his throat, "something that is not appropriate for a lady's ears."

Bea's eyes grew wide, and her head tilted as she looked out toward where Felicity was talking in a very animated fashion to her sister while clinging to Everett's arm.

"I saw both her and her sister in London," Graeme whispered near Bea's ear.

"Then, why did you ask me if they were both out?" She gasped as his lips brushed her cheek when she turned her head.

He smirked and shrugged. "I am a cad and wished to hear your opinion of them."

"Which I did not give," she pulled on her arm again, finally freeing it from his hold.

"Oh, but you did," he replied. "Your tone and the shortness of your replies told me all I need to know. You are not pleased with them — or more precisely, you are not pleased with Miss Love since she is the one who has enchanted my brother."

"I have never enjoyed my cousins," she refuted. "We have little in common. They like fashion and soirees while I prefer books and domestic pursuits. However, you have never been home when they visited before so you would not know how very unalike we are."

He chuckled. "Deny it if you must, but you are jealous." He climbed to his feet and extended a hand to her.

Bea looked at his hand warily.

"Come, you cannot sit here the full day. Mother will wish to know you took some exercise. She worries about you."

Bea's brows furrowed as she studied his face. "You will not say shocking things, and your lips will not touch me?"

A hint of mischief touched his smile. "You know I am constitutionally incapable of not saying something shocking at some point, but I shall refrain from touching any part of you other than your fingers with my lips."

Bea sighed and shook her head, but a touch of amusement curled her lips into a small smile as she placed her hand in his and allowed him to help her to her feet.

"Good heavens," he muttered as he pulled her upright, "if my brother does not marry you, I might. When you smile like that, it is difficult not to wish to break my promise to confine my lips to just your fingers."

He winked as her mouth dropped open. "As I said, I am constitutionally incapable of not being shocking." He tucked her hand into the crook of his arm.

He was teasing her, of course — at least, partially. She was both beautiful and beguiling, and were she not so obviously lovesick for his brother and were she not Bea, his friend and the closest thing he had to a sister, he would be hard pressed not to consider her as the next Lady Clayton.

Continue reading *His Beautiful Bea*

Acknowledgements

There are many who have had a part in the creation of this story. Some have read and commented on it. Some have proofread for grammatical errors and plot holes. Others have not even read the story and a few, I know, will never read it. However, their encouragement and belief in my ability, as well as their patience when I became cranky or when supper was late or the groceries ran low, was invaluable.

And so, I would like to say *thank you* to Zoe, Rose, Betty, Kristine, Ben, and Kyle. I feel blessed through your help, support, and understanding.

I have not listed my dear husband in the above group because, to me, he deserves his own special thank you, for without his somewhat pushy insistence that I start sharing my writing, none of my writing goals and dreams would have been met.

~*~*~

For those who might be interested in some of the topics touched upon in this book (such as coffee houses and the stock exchange), I have some of my research sources, along with some visual inspiration, pinned to a board on Pinterest. You can find that board at this link: bit.ly/Pinterest_Tom.

Other Leenie B Books

You can find all of Leenie's books at this link
bit.ly/LeenieBBooks
where you can explore the collections below

~*~

Other Pens, Mansfield Park

~*~

Touches of Austen Collection

~*~

Other Pens, Pride and Prejudice

~*~

Dash of Darcy and Companions Collection

~*~

Marrying Elizabeth Series

~*~

Willow Hall Romances

~*~

The Choices Series

~*~

Darcy Family Holidays

~*~

Darcy and... An Austen-Inspired Collection

About the Author

Leenie Brown has always been a girl with an active imagination, which, while growing up, was both an asset, providing many hours of fun as she played out stories, and a liability, when her older sister and aunt would tell her frightening tales. At one time, they had her convinced Dracula lived in the trunk at the end of the bed she slept in when visiting her grandparents!

Although it has been years since she cowered in her bed in her grandparents' basement, she still has an imagination which occasionally runs away with her, and she feeds it now as she did then — by reading!

Her heroes, when growing up, were authors, and the worlds they painted with words were (and still are) her favourite playgrounds! Now, as an adult, she spends much of her time in the Regency world, playing with the characters from her favourite Jane Austen novels and those of her own creation.

When she is not traipsing down a trail in an attempt to keep up with her imagination, Leenie resides in the beautiful province of Nova Scotia with her two sons and her very own Mr. Brown (a wonderful mix of all the best of Darcy, Bingley, and Edmund with a healthy dose of the teasing Mr. Tilney and just a dash of the scolding Mr. Knightley).

Connect with Leenie

E-mail:

LeenieBrownAuthor@gmail.com

Facebook:

www.facebook.com/LeenieBrownAuthor

Blog:

leeniebrown.com

Patreon:

https://www.patreon.com/LeenieBrown

Subscribe to Leenie's Mailing List:

Book News from Leenie Brown

(bit.ly/LeenieBBookNews)